# THE SALT LOSES HER
## Savour

## COLLEEN SMITH-DENNIS

LMH PUBLISHING LIMITED

Editor: K. Sean Harris
Cover Illustration: Courtney Lloyd Robinson
Cover Design: Sanya Dockery
Book Design, Layout & Typesetting: Sanya Dockery


Published by LMH Publishing Limited
Suite 10-11, Sagicor Industrial Park
7 Norman Road
Kingston C.S.O., Jamaica
Tel.: (876) 938-0005; 938-0712
Fax: (876) 759-8752
Email: lmhbookpublishing@cwjamaica.com
Website: www.lmhpublishing.com

Printed in the U.S.A.                                    ISBN: 978-976-8202-94-9


NATIONAL LIBRARY OF JAMAICA CATALOGUING-IN-PUBLICATION DATA

Smith-Dennis, Colleen
      The salt loses her savour / Colleen Smith-Dennis


      p. ; cm.
ISBN 978-976-8202-94-9 (pbk)


1. Jamaican fiction
I. Title

813      dc 22

# THE SALT LOSES HER Savour

*Ye are the salt of the earth: but if the salt has lost its savour, wherewith shall it be salted? It is thenceforth good for nothing, but to be cast out, and to be trodden under foot of men.*

**St. Matthew 5:13**

*Dedicated to all the people who have had their innocence and dignity inadvertently snatched from them. May they find the strength to rally back and continue their lives.*

**Colleen Smith-Dennis**

# CHAPTER ONE

## *The Salt*

*D*eidre-Ann took a final look at her outfit in the school's bathroom mirror. The blue, red and white, sleeveless blouse and skirt accentuated her slim, slight curves, and her long hair, tinged with brown and restrained by a pony clip, tickled her shoulders slightly. Two huge pert eyes stared back at her, their brown irises receding to the corner of her eyes, distancing themselves from the clear cornea. The eyes beamed with confidence and high self esteem, which were supported by the upright thrust of her shoulders and the unconscious firmness of her back. She pouted at the four freckles which had invaded her oval face since she was a toddler. No amount of wishing and cosmetics had faded or removed them. She had convinced herself that they were caste marks, but those which relegated her to the upper ilk of society. She smiled approvingly at herself and watched her thin lips spread to meet her dimples. She spun around to take in the total effect, smoothing her outfit as she did so. She was very pleased with what she saw.

She looked at her slender gold watch as she took her sports bag and headed for the auditorium. She knew that she was fifteen minutes late and would delay the start of the cheerleading practice, but that did not encourage her to quicken her gait. She walked at a moderate pace, enjoying the looks of approval and the whistles and calls of the senior boys.

"D-Ann, girl you ah happen!"

"Browning you look good! Bring me with you nuh!"

She revelled in the attention but pretended not to hear. She glided along unhurriedly, making certain to take the routes where most of the students could be seen. She even stopped twice to engage in brief conversation with two of her teachers.

When she arrived at the auditorium, everyone was waiting impatiently. She slowly placed her bag on a nearby table and then greeted everyone as if she were early. "Good afternoon people, glad to see you have all turned up for practice."

"But D-Ann, don't you know what time it is? And you were the person who warned us to come early," Michaela Marsh attacked her. "How come you always take so long to get ready?"

"This evening I have to finish early cause I have to take the bus," Tara McNeil added.

"Well, I had a few things to do," Deidre-Ann replied casually. "You know I'm involved in a number of activities, so sometimes, especially this evening, things don't run on time. Anyway, let us start," she added, dismissing the complaints.

The dream of the squad was to enter the International Cheerleading Competition, which was to be held in Florida in two months time. So far, the squad had done extremely well and had emerged runner up in the recently concluded National Cheerleading Competition. Deidre-Ann, whose specialty was to stand at the top of the formations and then spring to the ground in a graceful manner without falling or stepping out of line, was the star of the show. She had grown accustomed to the loud cheers, frequent praise and constant attention from the opposite sex. As usual, onlookers had gathered to watch them perfect their routine. The teacher who trained the squad was not always present and in her absence Deidre-Ann automatically took charge. This afternoon, she was in charge and was exulting in her authority as she gave orders, criticized, corrected and gave rare praise. "Sandy, if you twirl your pom-pom so slowly, everyone will think you're a senile old woman trying to remember where you are and what you're supposed to be doing!"

"Justine, you must sway to the music in time instead of moving to the one inside your head!"

"Tiffany, for God sakes keep still, don't create an earthquake or we'll all tumble to our deaths!"

That's right, she was enjoying every moment. "Shakira, your pacing is so on time!" The crowd which had gathered tittered at her every comment, even though she pretended to ignore them completely.

While she stood at the top of formation, she glanced around quickly to see if Con-Wayne Herald, the most acclaimed scholar and ace track star, was among the crowd watching her. She made him out just in time as he paused momentarily on the way to the schools' challenge room. She did her famous landing routine and raised her hands proudly to the sky.

"You are the salt of the squad!" someone shouted in admiration. "You are the star! It must go good with you in it!"

She did not acknowledge the praise but dismissed the squad, reminding them to be on time next afternoon.

As she took up her bag to leave, some of her classmates surrounded her. "D-Ann, you were just great, all of you! You are bound to come out on top in the contest."

"Oh, it was nothing, just hard training. I really hope I'll do well at the contest. I have to run now. I have a meeting with the planning committee for next week's barbecue. See you tomorrow." She dashed off this time instead of profiling. She had gained enough attention for one afternoon.

At that time of the day, there were not many people in the vicinity of the guidance counselor's office. Two ancillary workers were sweeping classrooms nearby and a few students were on their way from the playing field. She quickened her footsteps to a half run and rushed into the meeting which was already in progress. "Good afternoon," she greeted everyone and then sat down noisily.

"Hi Deidre-Ann," the teacher greeted her, smiling. "I thought you had forgotten about the meeting and there are so many things I want you to do."

"Sorry Miss, but I had cheerleading practice and the teacher was not there, so I had to take charge." The feeling of importance did not fail to surface in her voice.

"Okay, I understand. Did you remember to get the final word from Lyrical Vibes?"

"Yes Miss, they promise to be here by eight and have agreed to only play music appropriate for the occasion," Deidre-Ann answered, glad she had done her homework.

"That's good, and what about the other artistes, have they confirmed?"

"Yes Miss, all but Contemporary Bliss who will be touring Canada in that very week." Her voice had the ring of being well informed. The teacher ticked off some items on a list she had in front of her and continued. "Are you certain that Mr. Chapman will be prepared to be the emcee?" she asked, looking hopefully at Deidre-Ann, who again answered in the affirmative.

She then turned her attention to other aspects of the upcoming barbecue. Deidre-Ann listened half-heartedly now that the spotlight had shifted from her. Her mind roved to the outfit that she hoped she could persuade her mother to purchase for her. She wanted to be the best dressed person at the barbecue. She had to live up to her reputation of being a "hot girl". She looked on her watch and noticed that it was close to 5 pm. Her mother would be coming any time now and she was always impatient and complaining about her over-loaded afternoons. She had warned her that if she ever detected any falling off in her grades, she would have to unload all of her extra-curricular activities, especially since her major exams were only four months away. Deidre-Ann told her mother that she was worrying unnecessarily because she always studied every night, no matter how hectic her day had been. In addition to that, she was the top student in her grade and she intended to keep it that way. Brains, beauty and balance were sure to bring her results. She had everything going for her.

She asked to be excused from the meeting and hurried to meet her mother in the car park. By now the place was deserted and the only ones around were one of the ancillary workers and another man, a security guard, who had recently joined the staff. Deidre-Ann had seen him walking around the compound peering into the class-rooms and generally trying to familiarize himself with the compound. They were steeped in conversation and did not seem to notice her. She rushed past them and went to meet her mother.

On her way home, she could speak of nothing else but the barbecue. Her mother was used to her ebullience and rarely interrupted her, except to ask her what time the barbecue would be finished.

"Mummy, you know how these things are. They go on indefinitely and things really get exciting when the popular artistes are performing. If you miss that part it's like you didn't go the barbecue at all," she said animatedly.

"Yes Ann, I know what you're really trying to say, don't come for me until all the screaming, ranting and raving are over." She laughed loudly at her description of that particular genre of music. When she laughed, the close resemblance between mother and daughter was unmistakable, except for the four freckles and the youthful vivacity exhibited by Deidre-Ann. When it came to functions and her being in the spotlight, she was really effervescent.

She quietened down for the rest of the ride home. Her mind was filled with the excitement of going abroad for the cheerleading competition and the upcoming barbecue. If they won, not only would their school, Ingleglades High be lauded, but the squad would become even more popular, especially her, if she did her routine correctly. It would not be her first time going abroad, but this would be different.

"Mummy, can you please buy the pink and cream outfit we saw in Nairne's last weekend? I have absolutely nothing to wear to the barbecue." She turned to her mother with the most innocent and appealing eyes.

"Ann, has there ever been a time when you ever have something to wear to somewhere, or did not want a new outfit?" She looked at her daughter and shook her head in amazement.

"Mummy, you know how it is. Everybody watches to see what everybody else is wearing and it becomes big talk the day after the event. I would rather not go to the barbecue than wear something everybody has seen me in already." She said this in such a plaintive voice that one would have thought that she was discussing a sad matter.

"You young people and your false pride! Is there ever going to be an end to it? What will it take to make you all realize that there is more to life than fancy outfits and the glitz, glamour and glory of popularity?" Again she shook her head and implored heaven with her right hand. Her gold bangles shook as if in agreement with her.

"Mummy weren't you ever young and into things?" Deidre-Ann asked her mother, hoping that she would realize that she was no different from any other teenager. She looked accusingly at her, willing her to agree with the fact.

"Yes Ann, before anyone can get to forty, one has to be fifteen first, but when I was fifteen, I was not so taken up with clothes. I loved clothes but had to be content with what my parents could afford. There were six of us in comparison to two of you, and moreover we were more concerned about whether we would have enough money for food and school." She stopped speaking and concentrated ahead, not wanting to seem to be a preacher of the sermon too often.

"Oh mummy that was then, things and times are different now. You really don't expect me to live the same way you did, come on!" She looked at her mother incredulously as if she were from another world unknown to humans.

Her mother did not respond but had gone somewhere deep inside herself, maybe reliving difficult times, Deidre-Ann thought. She had no idea why her mother had to be so entangled in the sordid past. They were moderately well off, and for her, the relevant thing was enjoying life as best as one could without dragging the past along with you. She most certainly would make the most of the present and relegate the past to its rightful place, especially if it had nothing to do with her.

They were both lost in thought and did not notice the scenery as they drove past. They lived in a middle class suburban community which boasted large detached houses reclining in spacious comfort. The streets were devoid of potholes and the lawns, which extended to the sidewalk, were weedless and unruffled. Huge shade trees, evergreens, tamarinds and fichus, extended their bodies to protect the lawns from the venom of the sun. Many of the houses were graced by flowering shrubs which smiled broadly all year round. The quietude was often broken by the unbridled snarls of pedigree dogs which enjoyed a lifestyle akin to the social levels of their owners.

When they got to her street, Deidre-Ann got out of her mother's black 2010 Honda Civic to remove a stone which had appeared before the gate. She could not recall it being there when they had driven out in the morning. As soon as she had removed it, a voice called to her from across the road. It was Marla, a girl from another high school. "Hi Marla girl, ah jus' reaching in. I mean there is so much to do at school, it is not funny." She threw up her hands in mock despair.

"Well, I know you're always involved in everything or else they can't go on. The life of the party and all that, and ah know yuh enjoying the rush even though yuh complaining. By the way, when is the barbecue again?"

"You and your bird brain! Next week man, an' remember that you promise to come so don't bother with the foolishness! You can travel with me so it's not a problem." Deidre-Ann laughed at her friend's forgetfulness.

"Coming is not the problem, is what to wear. I have to find something hot so that ah don't look like a waif beside you. You're always so well dressed!" She looked at Deidre-Ann's cheerleading outfit which she had not bothered to change out of.

"Oh come on Marla, you can match me any day on any occasion so forget the modesty." She shook her head in disbelief at her friend's observation.

"We'll see. Catch you later, I hear my miserable little sister calling." She went inside and closed the gate without answering her sister.

Deidre-Ann went inside and her mother closed the gate behind her. She knew her older sister, Ashley, was not home from classes at the university yet, because her car was not there and there were no seventies and eighties oldies coming from her room. She loved her sister and often went to her room to curl up in her chair and talk with her, but sometimes she was too busy and did not have the time, so Deidre-Ann would retire to her room by herself and immerse herself in her studies. She didn't have much house work to do because the helper did almost everything, including cooking dinner. And there were only the three of them. Her father had allowed her mother to stay with the house and still sent money to pay their school fees. Her mother could hold her own because she was a chartered accountant. She did not bother herself too much about her father. When memories of the past with him came about, she simply pushed them away. She went to sleep and then woke up to study. When she went to sleep the second time, her sister still had not come home.

It was the night of the barbecue. Deidre-Ann and Marla were taken to school by Deidre-Ann's mother. On the way, Deidre-Ann noticed that the moon had hidden its face behind some grey disapproving clouds. The afternoon had been a fairly cheerful one with small active clouds racing around in wild abandon and the sun smiling approvingly at their antics. She was slightly surprised at the sudden change as she had heard no prediction of rain. She felt a sudden drooping of spirits as the thought of rain interfering with the barbecue assaulted her. She pushed the thought aside and got back into her positive mode. She even prayed a silent prayer.

The gloom pervaded for the rest of the journey and Deidre-Ann and Marla spoke endlessly by way of ignoring it. Deidre-Ann's mother did not join in the conversation but was immersed in her own private thoughts. She was driving fast as Deidre-Ann thought she should have been there already. When they were about two miles away from the school, there was a sudden bang and Deidre-Ann felt the car diving into a pothole. Her mother fought to control the vehicle as it wobbled right then left, and then swerved back to the right, out of control. Marla began screaming but Deidre-Ann could only cover her mouth. Mrs. Lenworth fought with the brakes and managed to bring the car under control just before it slammed into a tree.

When it came to a standstill, everyone sat silently for a while without moving or speaking. Deidre-Ann was the first to act.

"Mummy I think we need to see what damage has been done to the car." Her voice was devoid of the nervousness she felt.

Her mother flicked on the overhead light and searched the glove compartment silently for the powerful flash-light she normally carried with her. When she had found it, accompanied by the two girls, she went outside to assess the damage. There was not much done except to the left front tyre, which had fallen into the pothole. It was a bit soft but Mrs. Lenworth decided that she could still get to the school with it, if she drove slowly. One look around her surroundings had told her that this was not a place for one to be at that time of the night. The street lights were dim or had gone to sleep in some instances. Moreover, the street was peopled only by tall foreboding trees, which stood in askance, watching them indifferently from the sides of the road.

Mrs. Lenworth hurried the girls inside and drove off in measured haste. She focused intently on the road, watching out for troublesome potholes. She decided that after she had taken the girls to the school, she would stop at the gas station at the base of the hill and have one of the attendants deal with the problem. She felt a low feeling in the small of her stomach and attributed it to her near miss. Deidre-Ann and Marla were quiet for the rest of the way except when they were almost at the school. Marla spoke without warning. "I just feel like going back home, somehow ah just don't feel like going anymore, something not right!" Her voice held uncertainty and sounded a bit strange.

"Come on Marla, nothing much happened just now. Don't tell me you're nervous about a little accident. Don't let the excitement pass you," Deidre-Ann coaxed eagerly.

"Is just that ah get this weird unexplainable feeling all of a sudden, and ah don't think it's the pothole." She sounded confused and uncertain, which was uncharacteristic of Marla.

"Marla, let us put weird feelings behind and enjoy the now. It's not every day we get to have fun. Can't say I'm not shaken but I'm not going to waste my outfit and all of the planning. Moreover, everyone is depending on me to be there despite mishap or threat of rain," she ended, looking up at the vexed clouds, hanging encroachingly overhead.

"Alright then but ah think ah don't want to stay very late," Marla replied, pouting.

"Make sure you are ready by twelve when I get here Miss, and I certainly will not be walking around looking for you, so I hope you had charged your phone."

"Don't worry mummy, my phone is fully charged and if the big names do their thing early, I will be ready."

Deidre-Ann laughed and hugged her mother before she drove off.

She had timed herself well, a large number of students and visitors were already there and many heads turned in their direction.

"Lord have mercy! Dem girl yah a tek life, especially the one in the pink and cream outfit. She look good eeh man!"

"Boy she ah happen, really ah happen, is the salt in the pot this!"

Deidre-Ann felt pride burning her face at the heaped compliments. She was used to being complimented but she had not quite learnt how to handle the feeling of importance and exultation it gave her. She waved to everyone, smiling as if she was in a float parade being lauded for some national honour. She sweetly savoured the feeling as she made her way to the information desk to get instructions from the teacher in charge. The bellowing, screeching music which had stopped when she got to the gate started again, and groups of teenagers decked out in their latest style jeans, fashionable tops and decorated tee shirts, gyrated to the music, sketching the latest dance moves. Deidre-Ann watched them amusingly and then she felt a touch on her shoulder. She turned with a look of indifference on her face and stared into the eyes of an upper sixth student who was the captain of the celebrated chess team.

"Hi D-Ann, you're looking lovely tonight." He looked her up and down, taking in every small detail of her ensemble.

"Thank you," Deidre-Ann replied, feeling really good that someone considered so important in the school circle had found it fit to compliment her.

"Can we have a drink and a dance together later when things get more interesting?" he asked, looking at her expectantly.

Deidre-Ann hesitated before answering, not because she was making up her mind about whether she should, but to give the impression that she was not really too anxious. "Well, I suppose I can squeeze that in," she said hesitantly, as if she was working out things in her mind.

"Alright about tenish," he said, moving away, a satisfied smile growing on his face.

No sooner had he left, than Con-Wayne Herald came over. The school's top student and ace track star was dressed in trendy jeans and a blue polo shirt. Deidre-Ann pretended not to see him as he made his way towards her. She became extremely absorbed in the sheet with the lineup of artistes, and gave a mock start when he called her name.

"Oh hi Con-Wayne." She half turned to face him, still pretending interest in her list.

"I see you're busy as usual, always in the thick of things." He smiled engagingly at her, hoping for her full attention.

She gave one last look at her list and then turned to face him with a half interested look which did not register the pounding of her accelerated heart. "What's up Con-Wayne?" she asked casually.

"I was wondering if we could dance later on." The words came out in a rush.

Again Deidre-Ann took her time to answer. "Let me see." She did not want the time to clash with Tyrone's time. "It would have to be soon because I have to escort the artistes to their places when they come," she ended, importance rising in her voice.

"Okay, I'll be back in a little while then." He sounded pleased at her consent. When he left, Deidre-Ann smiled at herself. She was pulling in the big fishes and she knew a few girls who would not be happy about her catch.

She wandered around with Marla and a few of her friends for awhile, had jerked chicken, her favourite, and then went back and danced with Con-Wayne to a Trinidadian soca song loaded with sexual innuendoes. She would not have chosen that song to dance to but it was on when he turned up. He was a good dancer and she really had to pull out all her moves in order to keep up with him. Everyone gathered around them and cheered and whistled as they entertained them. Deidre-Ann really enjoyed herself and was a little sad when the music ended and she had to rush out to escort the first performer inside.

It was while the first performance was going on that she danced with Tyrone. It was not as good as dancing with Con-Wayne, but she still enjoyed it a little. Con-Wayne was there looking on and he did not seem very amused. Deidre-Ann smiled to herself, she was getting the attention she wanted.

By 12:30 a.m. all the artistes had performed and Marla, who was still feeling uneasy and tired, wanted to go home. Deidre-Ann looked at her watch and wondered why her mother had not called her yet. She wondered if the car was alright or if she was just giving her time to finish up. She got her things ready and was waiting with Marla when she got a call and said that she had to find Mrs. Munroe to give her some information. She told Marla to wait where she was and took her cell phone as she went in search of Mrs. Munroe.

# CHAPTER TWO

# The Salt Is Violated

"Marla is that you?" Mrs. Lenworth's irritated voice shouted at Marla.

"Yes Miss Lenny it is," Marla answered, happy to hear Deidre-Ann's mother's voice.

"Deidre not with you? I've been calling her for the past ten minutes and she has not answered her phone!" Mrs. Lenworth said angrily.

"I've been calling her too without an answer," Marla told her, starting to feel anxious.

"But weren't the two of you together? I don't understand."

"Yes Miss, we were standing here waiting for you to call and then she said she had to give Mrs. Munroe some information. She took her phone and left and I've been waiting here for her since and calling her but no answer," she summed up hurriedly, telling all she knew.

"Where are you standing Marla?" Mrs. Lenworth asked.

Marla described where she was and Mrs. Lenworth told her to meet her by the guards' station. As Marla walked towards the station, she asked everyone that looked like a senior if they had seen Deidre-Ann. Everyone answered in the negative. The feeling of foreboding which had been with Marla all night became greater. Most of the patrons at the barbecue had left or were leaving, and she expected Deidre-Ann to show up among them smiling and making excuses.

When she got to the guards' station, Mrs. Lenworth was outside in her car trying to convince the guard to let her in. Marla stood there for a while, watching them arguing and then Mrs. Lenworth drove in and parked. The look on her face was akin to blackened clouds. Marla was glad she was not in Deidre-Ann's place. When she was almost by Marla's side, Mrs. Lenworth went back to the car and came back with an umbrella. It was then that Marla felt the first drop of rain.

Mrs. Lenworth sprung into action as she came to stand by Marla. "I think the first thing we should do is to ask the people by the announcing booth to page her. If I remember correctly, the public address system is audible all around."

"I just hope they have not taken down everything in the auditorium yet," said Marla. "The music has stopped so they are most likely doing that now." Her voice was anxious yet hopeful.

They walked purposefully towards the auditorium, not bothering to stop and ask anyone about Deidre-

Ann's whereabouts. There were only a few people in the hall and as Marla had predicted, they were taking down the system.

"Sir," said Mrs. Lenworth urgently, stepping onto the stage. Her feet became entangled and one of the musicans quickly came forward to help her before she fell.

"Careful Miss, we don't want any accident. Jus' stand still an' let me get the cord from roun' your foot." He worked swiftly, moving the cord this way and that, and then Mrs. Lenworth was free. "Did you want to see anybody?" the musician asked, looking at the lady and deciding that she was not an ordinary woman.

"Sir, I can't find my daughter." Mrs. Lenworth got right to the point. "I've been calling her for some time now and she is not answering." Her voice was unsteady and filled with anxiety.

"Your daughter, what is her name?" He gestured towards her and the wings tattooed on the inside of his hands were exposed.

"Her name is Deidre-Ann Lenworth and she is a grade eleven student," she told him quickly.

"She is the girl who was escorting the artistes in, the one wearing the pretty pink outfit," Marla offered from the floor.

"Oh you mean the pretty browning, the one that everybody was looking at! Hot girl, real salt!" the musician laughed loudly. "Mummy ah see where she get the pretty looks from. Ah don't think you should worry, maybe she trying to force somebody not to take her home with them. Real hot girl dat, an' well active too." He laughed again and so did one of the other musicians on the stage who had overheard the whole conversation.

"Mister you seem to find this funny, but I don't! I came up here to ask you to make an announcement for me, not for you to have fun!" The stinging rebuke in her voice caused the man to turn full circle and look at her. She stared at him as if he was void of understanding and then without saying another word, he picked up the microphone from the floor.

"Attention, please! Please! Attention please! Will Deidre-Ann Lenworth meet her mother in the auditorium. I repeat, Deidre-Ann Lenworth, your mother waiting how long for you. Please report yourself to her in the auditorium now!"

Despite herself, Mrs. Lenworth almost laughed. Report herself indeed! She told him thanks and made her way gingerly from the stage, not wanting her foot to become entangled again. "I hope that the announcement will jerk her away from wherever she is," Mrs. Lenworth said stoutly.

"Well it was loud enough," said Marla. "This is just not like Ann. Ah wonder who she is talking to so long."

She thought of Deidre-Ann's dance mates, the two boys with whom she had seemed to have so much fun, especially the first one she had danced with.

They waited for ten minutes and no Deidre-Ann appeared. Mrs. Lenworth was pacing miserably, muttering to herself and calling her daughter's phone every minute.

"Now this is really serious Marla! Ann is not the type of girl to ignore my calls or refuse to cooperate with me. This is really serious!" Her voice had risen to a higher level and hints of panic came at Marla.

"I was thinking the same thing too," Marla said quietly. Her neck had begun to pain her from extending it to its full elasticity, looking in all directions to see if her friend would emerge with a shy smile and words of apology. She watched as the place became more and more deserted. The musicians had loaded their boxes and other paraphernalia onto their truck and were driving through the gate. Only a few persons who seemed to be waiting for rides were standing by the gate. One by one the lights on the school compound were being turned off and no wonder, it was almost 1:30 a.m.

"I think we should walk around and see if she is anywhere around," Marla said loudly. Her heart was doing a frantic dance and seemed to be bracing against her ribs, wanting to escape.

"But where are we supposed to look?" Mrs. Lenworth asked hysterically. "Where? All the lights are going off and a slight drizzle has started."

Marla stared out into the night and noticed the slight drizzle. "We need help to look for her. This is a big place and we don't know it very well."

"I think we had better explain the problem to the guards at the gate."

They explained their plight to the three security guards.

"Ah bet she gone with one of her friends dem," one concluded.

"Or maybe," started another, then he stopped, put his hand to his mouth and whispered something to the guard closest to him.

The guard laughed and said, "How you mean! Miss we can't leave the gate until everybody leave the compound and you see that the rain soon come down heavy, so you have to wait." His tone of voice suggested that he didn't see the urgency, that he honestly thought that the girl was somewhere having fun with her friends.

Mrs. Lenworth moved away from him, pulling Marla along as she did so. "Let us not bother ourselves with those idiots. All three of them do not have to man the gate when there is absolutely no traffic coming in and out. I will get somebody to help me." She opened her umbrella and dialed a number hastily. "Yes Nathan, it's me Carmelita, listen carefully I need your help right now. I'm at Ann's school and I can't find her anywhere. See if you can come and help me, do please." She ended the call and said to Marla, "I just spoke to my cousin Nathan, he is a detective, let these idiots here stay, he will come and help us." Her voice bore hope and confidence.

They went and sat in the car and waited for him to arrive. In about eight minutes, a police jeep turned up at the gate, horn honking impatiently for the guards to open the gate. One of the guards opened it, looking back at Mrs. Lenworth and Marla who were now standing in the drizzle, waiting anxiously to speak to Nathan.

Three plain clothes policemen stepped out of the jeep and Mrs. Lenworth and Marla walked towards them.

Mrs. Lenworth embraced her cousin and tried to explain. "They wouldn't help me," she said motioning towards the guards. "Say they can't leave the gate until everybody is gone. And I can't find her, do help me to look for her, do!" The tears in her voice were strangling her speech. She could barely get the words out.

"Alright Carm don't cry, we will find her. Don't cry. Everything will be alright. Security!" he bellowed, looking towards them disparagingly. "Which of you in charge?"

"Nobody special," answered the guard who had told Mrs. Lenworth and Marla they could not help at once.

"Why yuh need three big fools to stand up at one gate where nothing is happening and somebody here need help?" He looked as if he was about to hit the security guard who involuntarily backed away from him with a sheepish look on his face. "One of you who know the place well come with me and ah need to get the lights back on so we can see where we are going. Oh, and we need the keys to open the classrooms."

"The watchman have the keys," said one of the other guards. "Ah think him up by the kitchen section."

"Him a do what, eat when him suppose to be watching," one of the policemen said. "Nice watchman!"

The security guard called him on the phone. "Watchie, come here right now an' bring the key dem, the police want them." He hung up without waiting for an answer.

Two long minutes later, the watchman arrived breathless. His long face looked sullen and sleep popped out of his eyes. His mouth was covered up with a white substance which he tried to wipe away with the back of one hand. He was surprised to see the police officers and everyone else who had now gathered around.

"Night Watchie," Nathan greeted him without preamble. "I need you to open the classrooms and turn on the lights so we can search the place thoroughly. Come let's go right now."

"Who, who you looking for?" Watchie asked bewildered, wondering what this was about.

"You see anybody about the place except for the people by the gate?" Nathan asked, instead of answering his question.

"N-n-no Sir," the watchman stammered. "We cleared off everybody long time."

"Did you see a girl dressed in a pink pants outfit any-where around?" Mrs. Lenworth asked.

"Ah didn't really take any notice of anybody specially. Some of them was in corners all over the place and we clear them long time but ah didn't notice anybody special and ah don't think anybody would be in the classroom dem cause most of them did lock up from in the day." The sleep was gone from out of his eyes and voice, and his face seemed a little longer. Nathan's burly, tall figure and his stern aura seemed to have frightened him.

"We will go into two groups," Nathan said, taking charge. "The watchman will go with you officers and you will search the classrooms and the areas close by, and I will go with the guard and search the far grounds." He went back to the jeep for his umbrella and so did the other officers. Marla huddled under Mrs. Lenworth's umbrella as they both followed Nathan. He turned around and saw the persons who were standing by the gate following them and he sent them back. "Go back so that whosoever is outside can find you without trouble." He glared angrily. "Moreover we don't want any more problems than we already have." His severe, authoritative tone was loud in the wee hours of the morning.

On one accord, as on the day of Pentecost, they all turned back. The search began in earnest. All the class-rooms were opened and every corner peered into, the small dark openings between buildings were searched and so were the school grounds which were very extensive. The rain tried to hamper their movements but they were not deterred. Mrs. Lenworth and Marla were wet but they did not complain as the rain battered their feet and pressed their clothes close to their skin. Mrs. Lenworth had become very despondent. Her head was a beaten gong, and her heart no longer thumped and sought an escape, but had fallen out of its place low down into her belly where it had become dormant. She could no longer feel it. In its place there was a queer hallow of pain which had started to spread all over her chest.

There was a loud shout from the second party which killed the sound of the rain. It came at Mrs. Lenworth and Marla purposefully, unrehearsed and urgent.

"Dear God what is that?" Marla managed to utter.

Then it came again, loud, frightened, painful. "Over here! Over here!"

The group moved as swiftly as the sodden ground would allow, following the echo, behind the remotest building on the compound to the far end of a line of trees, behind the overburdened garbage skip, and the heap behind it. Mrs. Lenworth took one look at the heap and from somewhere inside her, a sound which could not be defined as a scream because it lacked the piercing quality; a sound guttural and undefined disturbed the rain, the night and all of nature. Mrs. Lenworth crumpled as a tyre which had a bad puncture. The sound of feet swishing and slopping in the rain, and voices, excited, mystified voices, and a small group of people, soaked and frightened, were brought to the spot by the eerie cry.

Marla, in her consternation, questioned, "Is she dead? Is Mrs. Lenny dead too?" When no one answered she cried out, "Tell me is she dead? Are they dead?"

Nathan and the other policemen, assisted by all three guards, tried to lift Deidre-Ann first, then Mrs. Lenworth. Deidre-Ann's pink and cream blouse, like a mockery of fashion, torn and caked with mud, was lying over half of her seemingly lifeless face and the pants had been ripped from her and were in tangled confusion at her ankles. Her body and clothes were spattered with mud. Once again, Nathan took command, almost choking with grief as the rain merged with his tears. "Put Mrs. Lenworth in the back of the car and one of you officers and her neighbour go with her. You will follow me in the jeep. The other officer, come with me in my jeep."

They struggled to the jeep with the females while the rain came down in a rage. No one spoke. The situation was too horrifying for words. Silent tears and shock had rendered all speechless. The main questions bombarding each person: Was Deidre-Ann dead? Who could have done such an evil act and why?

Nathan had no idea how he made it to the hospital. He deemed it an act of God that propelled him through the rain in the poor visibility. Sometimes he could barely see a foot ahead of him as the rain battered the windscreen and threw a frog in the throat of the horn. There wasn't much traffic at that time of the morning and maybe that was what saved him from an accident. The jeep, as if it had developed some ill will towards the driver, often wandered into the wrong lane and when corrected, it maliciously wandered off again. It behaved like that most of the time until they got to their destination.

As the two vehicles touched down at the Paul Beckford Hospital with horns screaming urgently, every unengaged person within earshot rushed out to see what the noise was all about. They watched silently as the policemen carried Deidre-Ann's still form into the casualty area, shouting for help. A few nurses and a doctor who were attending to patients in the area rushed forward, enquiring what had happened. Nathan tried to explain as the porters wheeled in a stretcher. They placed Deidre-Ann's inert form on it and whisked her away with the doctor and nurses running alongside it. By now Mrs. Lenworth had recovered, but was in shock. She was slumped in a chair just staring stupidly ahead; her vacant eyes fastened to the wall ahead of her. One of the officers spoke to one of the returning nurses who quickly beckoned to a porter. They placed her in a wheelchair and wheeled her to a nearby ward. Marla followed behind, wanting to see where they were taking her.

When they got to the ward, the nurse took her aside so she could give some particulars about Mrs. Lenworth and then she sent her back to the waiting area. Marla had been in contact with her family while on her way to the hospital but had completely forgotten about Ashley, Deidre-Ann's sister. She searched in her phone for the number and then called her four times before she got an answer. "Ashley, this is Marla. We could not get to you before but you need to hurry to the hospital right away." Marla's voice was sad and strained.

"Marla what happen, why do I need to come to the hospital?" She sounded sleepy and irritated.

"Something terrible happen Ashley, something terrible! We don't know yet if Ann is going to live."

"If Ann going to live? What yuh talking about? You're not making sense." The irritability had changed to bewilderment.

"Somebody attack her! Ashley just come! My parents are on the way. Your mother fainted and is in shock! Just come! We are at Paul Beckford!" She hung up, not wishing to prolong the conversation.

When she got back to the waiting area, her parents were there. She flew into her mother's arms and the tears gushed like a river in rebellion. Her mother allowed her to cry all she wanted to. Everyone in the waiting area was filled with curiosity. Two ladies and a gentleman bravely walked over and hesitantly asked what was the matter. After all, the doctor and nurses had abandoned them for their emergency, so it was only fair that they were appraised of the situation. In response to the question, Marla simply told them that her friend had been attacked at school and was badly hurt, and her mother had gone into shock. They went back to their seats and the news spread like an unchecked oil spill.

Marla and her parents went to sit a little away from the others. Marla, having gained a little control over her tears, spoke sadly to her mother. "Mummy somebody raped Ann! Can you believe it, somebody raped her! Her blouse was off and her pants were ripped up!" She spoke more to her mother than her father as she felt that discussing rape was a female matter.

"Are you sure Marla?" Mrs. Osbourne was horrified. Her eyes opened as wide as someone beholding an apparition.

"Yes mummy, raped her and who knows what else! Why would anybody want to do that to Ann, or anybody else for that matter?"

Her mother did not respond immediately mainly because anger was throttling her and partly because she was trying to find an answer to her daughter's question. The reasons for violating another human being have been age old questions which have been asked repeatedly. Sometimes explanations were offered and accepted, sometimes they were not. Mrs. Osbourne's mind could not provide an answer because horror had robbed her of logical thought. Moreover, she did not want to activate her thought process, it was too excruciating.

A little while later, a young lady walked into the waiting

area. She was accompanied by a young man who was about her age. The young lady bore a marked resemblance to Deidre-Ann. The pert eyes and the oval face were similar. The hair was dyed completely brown and was untidy, the wind having flung it in all directions. Her big eyes, made even bigger with confusion, seemed as if they were about to take leave of their sockets. Marla watched for a while as she stared around the waiting room.

"Hi Ashley," Marla shouted, forgetting where she was. "Over here!"

"Marla, do you remember where you are? You are not allowed to shout," Mrs. Osbourne remonstrated in a half whisper.

"Sorry mummy," Marla whispered back, beckoning to Ashley, who saw her and was striding as fast as a soldier on a mission towards her. Her tall companion with the twisted brown hair and drop earring in his left ear had difficulty keeping up with her. They hastily stepped over some people's feet, saying "excuse me" as they sailed along until they were beside the Osbournes, who had discreetly moved way to the back so they could talk in privacy.

Marla hugged Ashley tightly, transmitting her agony to her. "Ashley it is just awful, so awful. I just don't know how to explain!"

"Marla, please tell me what's wrong! I don't think I understand what you really said!" Tears accompanied her words. They raced down, stopped abruptly at her top lip and then dripped where the two lips met. Some found their way into her mouth, while some met and raced down her bottom lip and continued the journey down her chin. "Where is mummy and Ann? What happen to them?"

"Ashley, we were waiting at school for your mother to pick us up, then Ann said she was going to see a teacher and she did not come back." She stopped, too choked up to continue.

"What happened after that?" the unintroduced male companion asked.

Mrs. Osbourne looked at him and detected real interest. She continued where Marla had stopped even though she had not been on the scene herself. "The police later found her, way at the back of the school, unconscious. It seemed as if someone had attacked her, and done the bestial act of raping her." Mrs. Osbourne finished the hateful report, then burst into tears.

Ashley let out a high-pitched scream which aroused the attention of everyone in the waiting area. Her male companion grabbed her to him and smothered the second scream with his chest. He then hurriedly took her out-side. The Osbournes followed and together they checked the hysteria that was brewing.

Once they managed to calm her down, she started to make her way back inside. "I want to see them, I want to see Ann and mummy! They must let me see them!" The sobs started to rise again.

"Alright, I'll talk to the nurse, but you have to stop crying for awhile, Ashley," her male companion coaxed.

Ashley used her blouse to wipe her face and then went with her friend to speak to one of the nurses. She explained who she was and asked to be permitted to see her mother and sister.

"You can see your mother but you will have to wait until the doctors are finished with your sister, and if they say you can see her then so be it." She saw the pain in the girl's eyes and even though she was not unaccustomed to expressions of pain and grief in her job, her heart was pricked and she spoke softly to the girl. "They will be okay," she said, trying to reassure her.

"How can anyone ever be okay after being raped?" Ashley looked fully into the nurse's eyes as she waited for an answer. The nurse looked back at her and opened her mouth to respond but no words came. Ashley spoke slowly and deliberately to her. "When you take the salt out of something it has no taste, it loses its savour; when you violate a human's most sacred privacy what sense does life make anymore?"

The nurse looked at her again and offered no word of hope or comfort. Silently, she turned and led the way to her mother's ward. The Osbournes followed fearfully, hoping they would not be asked to turn back. The nurse seemed preoccupied and told them not to make any noise or stay too long or they might miss the doctor.

Mrs. Lenworth was not sleeping when they went into her room. She was sitting up and looking around her as if she was trying to determine where she was.

Ashley went up to her and hugged her, and the tears started to gush again. Her mother hugged her back, but looked at her indifferently at first, as if she did not quite remember her.

"It's me mummy, it's Ashley your daughter, look at me mummy, it's me!" She shook her, as panic got hold of her. "Mummy we need you to be here for us. I cannot manage this problem by myself, it's too big. I would never know what to do! Please mummy come back to us, Ann is not dead, she needs you to help her through to bring her back to life." She kept on shaking her until her male friend and the Osbournes pulled her away.

Mrs. Lenworth, as if she was coming back from a long, tiring journey, slowly looked around her. She looked at the faces without instant recognition and then she seemed to be seeing Ashley for the first time. "Ashley," she said faintly. "Ashley."

Ashley rushed towards her and hugged her tightly, almost suffocating her. "Mummy it's me! Yes it's me!" Her face was suffused with laughter which momentarily subdued the tears.

"Ashley." Mrs. Lenworth got out of the bed. "Ashley, where were you? I called you several times and you did not answer." She turned to look accusingly at the young man who was looking at them with a serious expression.

Ashley followed her gaze and hastily said, "No mummy, I was not out with Gerard. We were all working on a project and I was so tired I fell asleep."

Mrs. Lenworth continued as if she had not said anything to Ashley. "Ashley, somebody, some monster did a terrible thing to Ann. It's touch and go if she even lives. She was, she was..." Her sobs struck everyone in the nucleus of their heart.

Ashley hugged her mother and tried bravely not to cry. Someone had to be strong for the family, someone had to stand up and face whatever was coming. "It's okay mummy, she will come through, I know she will and one day somehow we will get to the bottom of this. Things can't remain hidden forever. Somebody must have seen or heard something." Ashley was trying to comfort her mother and give her hope that she did not feel.

As she stood there wondering how their lives would go on from there, the same nurse who had taken them to the room walked in hastily. "The doctor is asking for Deidre-Ann's family. Could you please come at once." She was surprised to see Mrs. Lenworth up. "I see you are feeling better now. That's good, come this way, don't keep the doctor waiting." She steered them past the waiting room into a small room lined with shelves of books, computers and single chairs. Two doctors were sitting around the table awaiting them.

"Good morning," the older of the two greeted them. His eyes were tired and sleepy, and his angular face had a short stubble of hair. "Which of you are the close family members?" he asked, surveying the six who had gathered.

"I am her mother and this is my daughter," Mrs. Lenworth said, pointing to Ashley. "The others are neighbours and a close friend."

"Okay, let me speak to you two first and then you can talk to your neighbours and friend afterwards."

The Osbournes and the young man went outside to wait.

"Alright," said the doctor as soon as the door was closed. "We have a sad situation here. As you might have guessed, your daughter was brutally raped. She is bleeding badly because her body is all torn up. Right now she is unconscious, suffering from blunt force trauma, that is, she was hit with something that does not have a sharp edge or point. These blows were delivered to the head and other parts of her body. She is still unconscious and might be for some time yet, but we are hopeful that she will recover in time. We are not certain yet if there is any serious brain damage. This we will find out as the days go by. We are watching out too for pneumonia because she was exposed to the rain for a while, we don't know how long. Right now all we can do is hope and pray and leave the rest to medicine."

The Lenworths stared at the doctor as if he had delivered a death sentence. No movement came from them, they might have been turned to pillars of salt or had suffered from Medusa's curse.

"Do you have any questions?" asked the second doctor who had not spoken before. His youthful gaze was filled with concern despite trying not to become emotionally involved in his patient's case.

"Do you have any idea how long she will be unconscious?" Mrs. Lenworth asked in a half-whisper. Her lips barely moved and the words seemed to have come from someone else inside her, rather than she herself.

"Not exactly, we hope she will come around soon. We are watching her closely and as soon as there are any signs of improvement, we will be sure to inform you." The young doctor hoped he could offer more comfort but he could not. They had to talk about what was evident.

"Can we see her now?" Ashley asked, wishing they would say no, as she really dreaded seeing her sister in her present condition.

"You can all see her for a few minutes but there should be no noise inside there. You must control yourselves. If there is any noise we will ask you to leave immediately," the older of the two doctors warned.

They showed the group of six to the room and warned, "Only for a few minutes now!"

Ashley held her mother's hand as she entered the room. Her feet were hesitant and heavy; they moved reluctantly and stiffly. She looked at her mother, but she was staring straight ahead, not wanting to meet anyone's gaze.

Deidre-Ann was in a room by herself. Ashley gasped and covered her mouth, mindful of the doctor's warning. She looked like a corpse, lying comatose with the white hospital linen draped over half her frame. Her face had a deathly still pallor. Her hair had lost its vibrant healthy look, and was limp and unkempt. Even the four freckles had lost their luster; they were barely visible and melted in with the general dullness of Deidre-Ann's appearance. The only thing which seemed to be alive was the intermittent drip of the intravenous device that was attached to her hand. Mrs. Lenworth gazed sorrowfully at her daughter and her nails dug painfully into Ashley's palm. Ashley winced, but still held her hand and kept her tears at bay. How had this happened to them, she questioned inwardly. People in her social strata did not just get raped like that. Things like that happened to care-less, carefree girls who made themselves too conspicuous and set themselves up for undue attention. How did her sister fall into that mode?

# CHAPTER THREE

# *The Investigation*

he following day, the police were at the hospital early. It was the same team which had assisted the family the previous night. They spoke with the doctor on the ward about Deidre-Ann's condition and wrote a detailed report of her condition. The information was the same as the family had been given. They asked to be allowed to see her and when shown into her room, stared dolefully at the inert form. They wondered if she would not be a vegetable if she survived and wondered who could have done such a dastardly act. Deidre-Ann's cousin was thinking differently, he vowed inwardly to find the beast and deal with him or them without mercy as Deidre-Ann had been dealt with. Anger and pain surged inside him, causing him to shake slightly. He turned away abruptly, not wanting anyone to see the heart-felt emotion of a police officer who was supposed to be as tough as the weathered rocks; a policeman who had seen many gruesome murder scenes and had been involved in many stand-offs with criminals.

He walked away and the others followed, noting the grimace on his face. They did not dare speak to him when he looked like that; they simply followed him to the jeep. He got in without telling them where he was going. He drove as if all of hell's fury had been unleashed and were chasing him to claim his soul. The others prayed silently that an accident would be averted.

He drove straight to the school which looked washed and dreary in the puny sunlight. He stopped and stared in an intimidating manner at the building as though willing it to reveal the evil secret of what had happened the night before. It stared back at him; cold, silent and unyielding. Nathan hit the horn furiously and continuously, causing the dogs in the nearby homes to add to his fury by barking violently and trying to push through the fence or jump over the wall.

A frightened looking figure emerged from behind the first block of buildings. As he walked he rubbed his eyes and tried to adjust his hazy vision to the jeep parked outside. It was the same watchman whom they had roused the night before. They had again roused him from his favourite past-time.

He approached the gate warily, rubbing his eyes and then widening them to aid his vision. "I wish somebody would pay me to sleep on my job!" Nathan hurled the comment sarcastically at the now wide awake watchman.

The watchman noted the somber look on the officer's face and wisely decided that a response to the specific comment would not be in his favour. Instead, he greeted him with mock cheerfulness. "Morning officer, how can I help you this morning?"

"It would be extremely useful if you stay awake long enough to open the gate," Nathan answered, glowering at him. "I can see how these terrible things can happen around here because those that should be watching and guarding are always sleeping. This is a lovely place to be!"

The sarcasm was not lost on the watchman but again he opted not to comment. The adage 'when you have your head in a lion's mouth take time and pull it out' came to him. If the police reported him to the principal he might lose his job, so it was prudent to ignore the comments and be as polite as possible. He opened the gate and bowed his head politely to the policeman who completely ignored his pandering.

Once they had parked, Nathan beckoned to him. "Show me the spot where we found the girl last night." It was a command, not a request, and the watchman led the way without comment. While they were on the way, Nathan requested the telephone numbers of the two security guards who had been on duty the previous night. On receiving them, Nathan called and told them to report to the police station where he worked. They both gave the excuse of being busy with affairs at home but Nathan warned them not to let him come and get them.

When they got to the crime scene, Nathan felt sick. There was nothing to be seen really except for the over-burdened skip with huge flies singing contentedly as they savoured the bits from the barbecue. There was no imprint of the spot where Deidre-Ann had lain in a heap the night before as the rain had eroded all traces. The officers walked around looking for clues, but there seemed to be nothing out of the ordinary except for garbage unwillingly pressed into the mud by the pounding rain. Nathan saw a rag lying near to where Deidre-Ann had lain. After staring at it for a while, he used a stick to free it from the mud. It was not all muddy; the section folded inside was clean. It was tawny with a line of small purple flowers; Nathan concluded that they reminded him of drooping sunflowers. He used the stick and pushed it into a black bag he had brought along for collecting evidence. He searched around for any blunt instrument which could be the weapon that had brought Deidre-Ann down, but his search yielded nothing. He looked around at the tall silent trees that had seen it all but were unable to divulge their secrets. *If trees could talk,* Nathan mused, *then everything would be revealed.*

"What exactly is your job around this place?" Nathan asked, turning to the watchman, trying to veil his searing pain and anger.

"Ah suppose to work from seven to seven," the watchman answered nervously.

"Besides sleeping, what did you do last night when the barbecue was going on?" Nathan scrutinized the watchman's face.

"I walk around all over the compound." He used his hands to show the extent of his walking.

"Did you come around this area at all?" Nathan peered at him closely, anxious to hear what he would say.

"Yes one time, but nobody was roun' here and nobody hardly come roun' here so, because it dark and anything can happen. The light don't really turn on roun' here so. I don't know what the little girl was a do roun' here." He looked perplexed as if he was really trying to figure out the mystery.

"I don't believe you came anywhere near here at all!" Nathan shouted at him. "You look like you 'fraid of even you own self!"

"As ah say, ah come roun' here one time an' the late time dat the fair over ah don't know what anybody would be doing roun' here so. They should be making for their yard," he said in his defence, pouting to show what he thought of anyone who was foolish enough to go into a dark area.

Nathan looked at him and decided to leave him alone for the time being. He walked back to the jeep and drove to the station without speaking. He was absorbed in another world and the quiet conversation of his colleagues did not pique his interest.

He had to wait for another hour before the two security guards arrived at the station. They seemed to have met each other at a central point and Nathan wondered what story they had concocted between them. He questioned them separately and both stuck to their story of doing their rounds but staying mainly among the students and other patrons in order to maintain peace and have things going smoothly. The security guard who had been employed only a week earlier at the school said he did not know the grounds very well and had not gone around the area where Deidre-Ann had been found at all. He too wanted to know why Deidre-Ann had gone around that area. He looked at Nathan suggestively and Nathan gave him an icy stare which caused his body to quiver slightly. He immediately assumed a serious expression which came with the realization that Nathan was not someone to play with.

Nathan sent them away feeling that there was something he had neglected to ask them but he could not remember what it was. He decided he would question them on Monday when he went back to the school to do more investigation.

Monday morning dawned bright and cheerful. Small, soft white clouds romped frivolously in the indulgent pale blue sky. Following the deluge of the previous Friday into Saturday morning, the green things of nature looked scrubbed and revitalized. Minute buds forcefully freed themselves from bondage and pushed their tightly folded bodies forward, drinking in the free fresh air which nature afforded. They gave no thought to the fact that after a few weeks, their glory would be lying at their feet, returning to the substance from which all life form is derived.

No one at Inglesglades High stopped to look at nature or reflect on its ongoing schedule on this particular morning as excited and subdued chatter swept the compound.

Like Noah's flood, it rose and rose until almost everyone was swept along in the widening wave of gossip. The details were not distinct but the basics were established: Deidre-Ann had been raped and beaten behind the school and was fighting for her life in the hospital. Gossip had it that it had occurred after most people had left the compound. Gossip also had it that more than one persons was involved. The endemic gossipers also started speculating about the perpetrators and their motives. No one laughed openly, but a few claimed to have seen it coming. All the female teachers and her classmates wept. Although crying was not thought to be a male trait, there were some wet eyes among the males, especially the older ones.

Worship was flat and uninspiring. The teacher in charge seemed more to be carrying out a necessary hurried ritual rather than seeking to really worship God. The only indirect mention of the occurrence was in the prayer by the head boy. He beseeched God to heal the wounded hearts, bodies and spirits of all those who had been wronged and those who were mourning, and allow His sure brand of justice to be swift and rewarding. There was no mention of the barbecue in the hasty announcements after prayer, and both teachers and students marvelled that worship had finished on time for the first time in a long while.

Classes started on a low ebb, many students only wanted to discuss the incident but the teachers skillfully steered them away from the topic, pointing out that only pain would result in such a discussion.

As the morning advanced, fierce whisperings started among the students. The police had arrived and a number of boys had been summoned to sit outside of the principal's office, which was being used to conduct the interviews. The boys sat in the company of two police officers. This gave them no opportunity to communicate or corroborate alibis. The two boys that Deidre-Ann had danced with, Con-Wayne and Tyrone, were also among those to be questioned. They looked as frightened and uncomprehending as the other members of the basketball team who it was rumoured on that black Friday, were standing the closest to the back of the school with a number of girls.

They were questioned separately by Nathan and another detective who had been drawn into the case only that morning. Before questioning, each file had been pulled and skimmed through.

The first one to be questioned was Con-Wayne. He decided that he had done nothing wrong and would put his nervousness away and answer directly. The officer accompanying Nathan launched into the questioning. He assumed an aura of austerity and professionalism. His balding head and thick lips added to his strict appearance and made Con-Wayne pray inwardly never to come face to face with him again. The low threatening voice did nothing to dispel his prayer.

He politely greeted Con-Wayne and offered him a seat. Then he asked, "What is your name?"

"My name is Con-Wayne Herald," Con-Wayne replied politely.

"How old are you?" The officer sat back and looked indifferently at the boy, trying to sum him up.

"I am sixteen years old."

"Are you in the same class as Deidre-Ann? "

"No, Sir, I am not." His answers were complete and well formulated.

"How did you get to know her?" The officer looked intently at Con-Wayne as if he was asking him if he had committed the crime.

"She is a popular person in the school because she is involved in cheerleading and other planning activities. It was only a few weeks ago that I introduced myself to her. We are not really friends, more like acquaintances."

The detective listened to the cultured voice of the school's top student and although people could be very deceptive, decided that this one did not seem to be a potential criminal. He pictured him walking the grounds of a university in a gown. "I understand that you created quite a stir dancing with her on Friday night."

Con-Wayne smiled shyly before answering. "I really do enjoy good dancing. I asked her to dance with me and she agreed. We really had a good dance." He was unapologetic, he had really enjoyed himself.

"Where did you meet afterwards?" The detective was trying to destroy his composure and confidence.

"Sir, I did not tell you I had gone anywhere with her, because I hadn't and nobody can tell you they saw me with her after the dance! We danced and that was it!"

The officer looked at the earnest young face in front of him, realizing he could not catch this one out. "What time did you leave the barbecue Con-Wayne?"

"About twelve, my father came for me and I went home. Tyrone and Hedley also got a ride with me," he added, remembering that Tyrone was waiting outside to be questioned.

"Do you remember seeing anyone moving around with Deidre-Ann?"

"What do you mean by moving around?" Con-Wayne asked.

"I mean walking around with her most of the time." Slight irritation tugged at his voice, he was not accustomed to being questioned.

"As far as I remember Deidre-Ann was not moving around with anyone special. She was responsible for escorting the artistes in and out and I suppose that kept her very busy. Moreover, I was not where I could see her all the time, I went around with my friends, eating and having fun." His answer was precise but unrehearsed.

"Do you know anyone who has a grudge or does not like her?"

The question took Con-Wayne off guard. He thought for a little while and then he answered. "Sir, everyone has enemies." He looked directly at the detective and repeated, "Everyone has enemies. Sometimes you create them by being different and being good or excellent at things. Sometimes you are singled out because of something that is not your fault; maybe because of your race, religion, antisocial behaviour and as some label it your so-called sexual orientation." The officer visibly widened his eyes at the last one on the list. Con-Wayne continued, "Deidre-Ann was popular, that could have created enemies. But that kind of envy is usually among girls, not boys. I really do not know who her enemies are." His meaning was clear; the detective looked at Nathan, shook his head and dismissed Con-Wayne.

When he was gone, Nathan commented, "That is a really smart young man. Heaven help us if he decides to get on the wrong side of the law, we would really have problems!"

They interviewed the other boys and learnt nothing except from Paul Rose. Nathan was the one who was interviewing him.

"Paul, do you know anyone who does not like Deidre-Ann. Anyone who would have wanted something bad to happen to her? Think carefully now, what was the reaction at school this morning? What are the children saying and who seems not to care that she is hurt?" Nathan peered closely at Paul, hoping to draw him out, hoping to get even a faint idea of who might be responsible.

"Well, Sir," Paul started after thinking for a while. "Ah wouldn't exactly say that they hate her, but some of the girls in her class think she boasty and show off."

"Girls like who?" Nathan asked. "Just tell me the names of a few of them."

"Girls like Jo-Ann Levy, Tamika Neale, Terrina Gayle." Paul had a finger on his bottom lip as if that could aid his memory.

"And what about the boys? Which ones were attracted to her? Which ones would like to be more than just ordinary friends?"

Paul thought for a while and then said, "As far as I know all the senior boys wouldn't mind being her boyfriend because she really did look good and Michael Bent who plays cricket would give anything for her to notice him." He felt like a traitor adding the last bit of information because that was just talk among boys, but the piercing, probing eyes of the police seemed able to loosen one's tongue like the effects of alcohol.

The interview with the girls yielded nothing much but petty grudges born of the belief that Deidre-Ann always tried to take over everything and always wanted to be in charge as if nobody else had ideas but her. Tamika Neale expressed the idea that because she was brown she thought that she was the most attractive girl in the school and dressed and showed off so that every-one could see her. When Nathan asked her if Deidre-Ann had ever told anyone these things about herself, Tamika admitted that she had not but just the way she went on was enough for anybody to see this.

Nathan commented, "So you really don't like her at all, what do you think about what was done to her?" He almost added, as another woman, but stopped himself.

"Sir, I think you get me wrong," Tamika started in response to the question. Her face was serious and her eyes blinked unwillingly as she spoke. Nathan could not ascribe any particular emotion to her as she continued.

"I am a girl and what happen to her can happen to any girl at any time so nobody in their right mind could feel good about this. We only never expect that this could happen to somebody like her and right here at school. Don't get me wrong officer, as far as I know everybody feel bad whether she boasty or not. None of the girls are happy cause every day we hear about things like this, and if it can happen to her it can happen to us too, especially those of us who have to take the bus and taxi all the time!"

This time, the police officer heard the pain. She had said it quite realistically; it could happen to any female.

The last person to be interviewed at the school was Mrs. Munroe, the teacher Deidre-Ann had gone in search of. She, like all the boys, was surprised when she was summoned. All the teachers stared at her, wanting to know how she had got involved. She shrugged her shoulders nonchalantly and then made her way to the principal's office. Her heart was doing a strange uneven pounding which happened only when she was nervous or stressed. She decided she was not stressed and questioned what she was nervous about. She had no information that would help the police, of this she was certain, so why should she be nervous.

Nathan greeted her with a smile and offered her a seat. He was not certain what to make of the medium height, Chinese woman with the small round eyes. "I am sorry to disturb your schedule but I just need to talk to you for a little while about Deidre-Ann."

"That's okay officer, I hope I can be of help although I don't see how." Her voice was low and unemotional.

"Mrs. Munroe, am I correct?" Nathan asked.

"Yes, you are," Mrs. Munroe affirmed.

"Which subject do you teach Deidre-Ann?"

"I do not teach her," Mrs. Munroe said, not offering more than she was asked.

"What then is your relationship with her?"

"She is a member of the Interact Club, which I am in charge of."

"Okay, I understand now." The questioning frown disappeared from Nathan's face. "How involved was she in the planning for the barbecue?"

"She was very involved. Deidre-Ann is always fully involved in planning activities. She's the life of anything she is involved in. It was her job to escort the artistes to the performance area and she did a good job of it." Mrs. Munroe was warming up a bit; she seemed a little more comfortable.

"On the night of the barbecue did you speak much to her?" Nathan wanted to find out.

"Yes, I did. I had to give her instructions about several things," Mrs. Munroe replied.

"Can you remember about what time you last spoke to her, Mrs. Munroe?"

"It was about 11:30 when I had to leave," Mrs. Munroe recollected.

"11:.30!" Nathan was surprised.

"What, why are you surprised? I left at 11:30, that's when my son came for me, said he had to study and had to leave at once." Mrs. Munroe looked from Nathan to the silent police officer.

"Mrs. Munroe, did you tell Deidre-Ann when you were leaving?" Nathan questioned.

"As a matter of fact, she carried a box to the car for me," Mrs. Munroe replied, perplexed.

"Mrs. Munroe, at approximately 12:30 or there about, it was reported that Deidre-Ann got a call and hurried off saying she had to find you and give you some information." Nathan looked directly into Mrs. Munroe's eyes, willing her to dispute what he had heard.

"Officer, not only was my son in the car with me, but Mr. Grey, one of the security guards, also came to the car when I was leaving. The canteen manager had asked him to give me a bag. Before I drove off, Deidre-Ann went back towards the auditorium and it was certainly not twelve thirty." Mrs. Munroe was adamant about the time. "And I did not call Deidre-Ann or anyone at school for that matter!" Mrs. Munroe was looking at the officers, aghast at what she was hearing.

"This is certainly strange, Mrs. Munroe, certainly strange. It seems as if someone used your name to lure Deidre-Ann away to some meeting place. Her friend, Marla, said she got a call and left saying she had to meet you to give you some information." He repeated the information slowly, trying to make sense of it.

"That makes no sense officer because I left the compound and if you don't believe me, you can check with the security guard and also find out from anyone at the gate if I was seen on the compound after I left."

"We will most certainly check out everything of interest that we find out here today. Before you leave I would like you to make a list of all the artistes and other musicians who performed at the barbecue. I would like to interview all of them."

When Mrs. Munroe left, Nathan and his colleague sat in silence for a while trying to digest what they had learnt. It wasn't much but they had learnt a few interesting things.

# CHAPTER FOUR

# Deidre-Ann Wakes Up

Mrs. Lenworth looked at Talk Waves, Deidre-Ann's parrot, half heartedly clutching to the bars of its cage. It had been neglected for the past four days as there was no one around to really care for it. Mrs. Lenworth wondered if it was still alive. She pushed her fingers through the bar and poked it. It made a faint squawking sound and slowly disentangled itself from the bars and moved freely to the other side. She tried to talk to it. "Hey Talk Waves, how are you?" There was no response except for a faint squawk. "Hey Talk Waves, how are you? I know you miss Ann." At the mention of Deidre-Ann's name, Talk Waves lifted his head a little and looked around. Mrs. Lenworth continued to talk to it. "She's not here. Don't know when she will be. I hope it will be soon."

The bird leaned its head to one side as if it was listening and then flopped its head on its chest of green and yellow feathers as if it had lost interest in the conversation.

Normally when the occupants of the house were speaking to him and stopped in mid conversation, Talk Waves would have said "Talk! Talk! Tell me." But today it said nothing. Deidre-Ann had been its owner for the past two years. She had asked her mother to buy it for her as a birthday present. She had named it from one of her favourite talk shows and had trained it to talk. Soon it became everybody's pet and they all had to be careful what they said around it.

Mrs. Lenworth took the parrot out and cleaned its cage. It stood in the make shift cage the entire time and did not make a sound. When she was almost finished, Ashley came out to the back porch. Her eyes were red and puffy from lack of sleep. The dark circles under them resembled smears of black lipstick. She sat lackadaisically in the three seater lounge chair and folded her legs beneath her. She looked without interest at her mother carrying out the chores and then she called to Talk Wave. "Hi Talk, what's up? You're unusually quiet this morning." The parrot turned its head in her direction and made a puny squawk. "Well, cat's got your tongue, you're about as cheerful as the sky outside!"

Mrs. Lenworth turned her face upward and the un-friendly sky stared back at her. "We sure are going to get some rain this afternoon. I think it's time we start getting ready to go to the hospital." Her last few words got caught in her throat as she hastily put back the parrot in its original cage and placed some food and water in it.

Ashley did not respond, for a while she had gone to another place in her thoughts. As her mother was moving away she cleared her throat and called her back. "Mummy, I need to talk to you."

Mrs. Lenworth stopped and turned towards her daughter. Her eyes were sunken and tired and her nose seemed more prominent than ever because her face had become so drawn and lined over the past four days. "Yes Ashley, what is it?"

Ashley cleared her throat again and then as if searching her mind for the right words, said in a quiet voice, "Mummy I know this is going to hurt but I think we should find a way to tell daddy what has happened to Ann."

For a long moment Mrs. Lenworth stood as if she had not heard her and then she gave her a searing look. "I thought you were intelligent enough to know not to bring up such a distasteful subject."

The mordant response struck a bitter chord in Ashley's heart. She knew she had entered turbulent waters but still she plunged ahead. "Mummy, I understand the pain and bitterness."

"You most certainly do not, or else you would not even bring up that topic in this house!" The bitter, biting tone cut Ashley short.

"Mummy even though you might not believe it, but I am your daughter and I am hurt too, but in times like these, the family needs all the support it can get from every single family member. We need to stand together to help Ann get through this, if she can!" Her words were earnest, sincerity rang in her voice.

"When that man was here years ago, did he stand up for this family? Answer me; did he stand up for this family?"

She was edging closer to Ashley and she feared she would grab her and hit her.

Ashley shifted uncomfortably in the chair. "Calm down Mummy, please. I know what we are all going through and what you have gone through and even though you don't seem to believe it, what I went through. Ann was the only one who did not seem to make it bother her much. Maybe she was too young to understand the full impact of what happened. I am just saying he is still her father and should at least be informed about her condition."

"Well since you want to inform him, find him and do so, it would be interesting to see if you can find him. But one thing I want to warn you about..." She went up and bent over Ashley who recoiled in fear. "When you find him, keep him to yourself. Do not dare bring him anywhere near the rest of this family." She stomped off in such anger that Ashley was certain that the tiles had been damaged.

She did not want to infuriate her further, so she got up and went to get dressed to go to the hospital. As she dressed, she tried to block out her mother's face. That was the face she had worn the night her father had left, seven years before. A face that had been acrid and twisted. A face filled with venom and hatred. A face bearing pain and suffering. She had never forgotten that face or the loud, harsh quarrel which had pulled their neighbours out of their houses and placed them in their yards, exclaiming as they digested the tidbits of the searing quarrel thrown to them in the night air.

She cleared her mind and decided that since her mother did not want her father around, she would not be the one to introduce him back into their lives, and besides her mother was right, where would she find him?

When they got to the hospital, several family members were already there. Mrs. Lenworth had tried to contain the news but somehow it had spread and more and more family members, mainly on her side, came or called to hear what was happening. The nurse kept them from seeing Deidre-Ann so they had to be satisfied with second-hand information.

That day when Ashley and her mother went to visit Deidre-Ann, there was a change. There was a cluster of medical officials around her bed. When the two rushed forward to see what was happening, they were surprised to see Deidre-Ann's eyes open. They called out her name and rushed forward but they were held back.

"You have to be very quiet so that you don't frighten her," warned one of the doctors. "Her eyes are open and she can hear us but when the voices become loud she closes her eyes. She has not responded in words to any of us yet. Maybe when she sees your faces she will respond a little but be very quiet and gentle with her." He made way and allowed them to go to Deidre-Ann.

Mrs. Lenworth reached forward and gently took Deidre-Ann's hand. She called her name but she only stared unblinkingly at her. Her hands felt cold, moist and limp. Mrs. Lenworth wanted to ask the all important questions: Would she be normal again? Would she ever be able to be Deidre-Ann, bubbly Ann again?

The same thoughts were afflicting Ashley. As she watched her sister's open but blind eyes, she thought it would have been much more humane, if she had died. A mindless person who would only be a shadow of herself would be better off at another place where mindlessness and sickness were of no account; where the searing gossip would be stilled forever; where the tumult of the heart would cease and there would be peace, perpetual peace, peace until judgement day. The tears cascaded down her face and would have continued their down-ward rush had they not been blocked by her blouse. She turned away and bumped into one of the doctors. She lifted her eyes to concerned eyes, eyes that had grown accustomed to suffering but were not indifferent to it. He gave her a comforting look but did not try to stop the tears as he knew that they, in themselves, could help in the healing process.

Their relatives waiting outside were elated that there had been a change. They envisaged rapid recovery but Mrs. Lenworth and Ashley did not share the optimistic feelings so they kept quiet, squeezing out a little smile every now and again, forced smiles, smiles that were facades of hidden hurt and hopelessness.

Two days later, Deidre-Ann showed more signs of life. She was now able to sit up and talk a little, but every time one of the male doctors entered the room, she started screaming and covering herself from head to toe. The nurses got a different response, they were able to talk and attend to her, but she would not allow anyone to bathe her. Several nurses had to hold her in order to carry out this activity. When Mrs. Lenworth and Ashley were told about this, they offered to carry out the activity themselves. This too did not satisfy Deidre-Ann, she just looked at them without recognition and fought fiercely.

A week later, the doctors had a meeting with the Lenworths. The chief resident started by giving a report of Deidre-Ann's condition from the time she had been admitted to the hospital until the time of the meeting. At the end of the report, he cleared his throat and looked directly at the mother and daughter. "I called this meeting not just to give a report but to make a particular recommendation." He stopped and searched their faces for a reaction and seeing none, he continued. "I know that this is unpleasant, but under the circumstances, my team and I generally feel that your daughter would benefit more from psychiatric therapy. Right now it's not just amnesia or loss of memory. She has lost touch with reality. This is a result of the savagery she has experienced and also because of blows she has received to the head. She still needs to be treated for the physical, but the mental is more urgent."

A subdued sob came from Mrs. Lenworth and she covered her mouth. Ashley cried openly, not bothering to stifle the tears.

No one spoke for several seconds and then the doctor continued. "We have here a list of recommended hospitals and private care centres. The ones both public and private that we have ticked are the most highly recommended but the one you choose depends on affordability and access." He looked from one to the other and then threw in a few words of comfort. "I have seen much worse cases than this and somewhere, somehow, and I really think it's by divine intervention, healing is wrought. I believe in the science of medicine, but there are some things such as troubled minds that medicine does not heal. If you believe in the Almighty there is no telling what miracles your faith can wrought. I tell you, I have seen it. You need to make a decision in the next few days and tell us so that we can carefully appraise the doctors in charge of the situation. In the meantime, expect some weird behaviour from your daughter, but remember in every-thing to be patient and kind. She will get worse before she gets better and it will not exactly happen overnight. Are there any questions that either of you would like to ask?" He looked from one to the other expectantly.

It was Ashley who spoke up. "Do you really think she has a chance to recover both physically and especially mentally, or are you just selling us false hope?" She looked from one to the other, trying to read their minds or to see whether the truth could be garnered from their expressions.

The only female doctor in the team answered, "I would hope the doctors are taken seriously by everyone. I think I can speak on behalf of my colleagues and say that we are realistic and speak honestly about what we believe. Remember the words of Doctor Wisdom here, patience, kindness and divine intervention are essential ingredients in this healing process." She sat back in her chair and looked straight ahead.

Following the meeting, mother and daughter went outside and sat in the car. There was no need for words, their tears told it all. It was Ashley who recovered first.

"Mummy we have to be strong for Ann. We cannot allow the doctors to have more faith than we do. We have to make our choice and work along with the system."

Mrs. Lenworth tearfully nodded her agreement and together they examined the list of psychiatric care facilities given to them by the doctor. They called Nathan and informed him about the developments. Ashley felt that now more than ever they should try and get in touch with her father. While he had lived with them, Deidre-Ann was his favourite child. On the rare occasions when he was home early, he would read to her and they would talk about all kinds of childish things. She had even got him to put on one of her television character costumes and together they had romped from room to room, upsetting the furniture and displeasing his wife who had eventually locked them in the garage. It was strange that she should remember him at a time like this because he had caused great sadness in the family and this was a time of profound sadness. She wisely did not mention any of her thoughts to her mother as she did not want a rift to develop between them. It was enough that she had angered her a few days before. She knew what she was going through and had no intention of causing more suffering.

On the day that Deidre-Ann was to be removed from the hospital, Nathan came to assist the family. He watched helplessly as the hospital officials tried to get Deidre-Ann to leave the ward. She kicked and spat and shouted, "Don't touch me! Put down your stick! Your hands are dirty! Don't touch me!"

After they managed to restrain her, the doctors instructed the nurses to put her in a straitjacket. Ashley could not help the tears from escaping when she saw the mindless robot that her sister had become. She did not recognize them and when her mother tried to get close to her, she bit at her and shouted, "Don't touch me! Your hands are dirty!"

When they finally managed to get her into the ambulance, the doctor gave her an injection and the scary screaming subsided. Her head lolled back on the stretcher and she looked like a strange creature from a place undecided. Ashley, who was travelling in the ambulance with her, hit herself in the face trying to determine whether she was awake or not. She wanted someone or something to shake her out of the nightmare. She was sure that none of what was happening was real. The screeching tyres and the screaming horn of the speeding ambulance added to the surreal quality of the whole experience. At one point Ashley pretended that she was standing by the roadside and seeing the ambulance flitting past, wondering what the hurry was and whether anybody was really ill or was it that the driver just wanted to show his dominance of the road. She watched all the vehicles pulling aside to facilitate the ambulance and then when Deidre-Ann made a sound, her attention was drawn back inside and reality grabbed her when she looked at the stiff figure with the head thrown to one side like a dead bird. She stifled a surging sob by pressing hard on her mouth.

They reached the Serene Comfort Hospital within an hour. The institution was a fifteen minute drive from the city. It was a private institution occupying approximately ten acres of land. The large facility was set in the middle of the property so there was space all around. The grounds outside lived up to its name; there was the absence of the usual constant hospital activity. The security was in place and only two nurses and a doctor were seen walking hurriedly along, chattering and laughing. There were large colourful gardens set aside from the parking areas. Each garden had large shade trees and some boasted fountains which added to the soothing serenity of the environment. The grass was green and closely shaven, and there were picket fences around select plants. Rising from the ground, under all the shade trees, were stone benches. Ashley felt like lying on the grass and allowing the water to play all over her body, maybe then she would wake up from her nightmare.

They brought Deidre-Ann into the hospital, still heavily sedated. Ashley did not have time to take note of the interior as her help was needed to get Deidre-Ann settled into her assigned room. It was a fairly large room and was painted a restful shade of pink. The windows were board louvers and there were no curtains. The room was sparsely furnished with a small bed and a bed-side table, a chest of drawers and a chair. A ceiling fan which was churning away cooled the room a little. There were no decorations of any sort, it was just stark.

Ashley enquired about this from the nurses, who were trying to make Deidre-Ann comfortable. They had removed the straitjacket and were tucking her in. The nurses told Ashley that patients were not allowed things with which they could hurt themselves. Curtains were not allowed because they could be torn down and used destructively; mirrors could be smashed and used as a lethal weapon; crochet could be swept off the furniture and used in a harmful way; stainless steel cutlery and breakable plates, cups and glasses were simply not allowed; so too were electronic and other gadgets. Ashley stared at the nurses as if they had just told her that Deidre-Ann would not be allowed to live.

When the nurse saw the consternation on her face she laughed and said, "Anyway this young lady will not need most of those things right now. Our chief job now is to get her back into the world."

Ashley agreed with her on that score. The nurse gave them a visiting schedule which she told them should be strictly observed. The hospital did not encourage anything that would disturb its programme.

When they were ushered out, Ashley noticed that there was a tall burly man seated at her sister's door, and the nurses were sitting in what must be one of the nurses' stations which seemed to be central to the other rooms on that side of the hospital.

While her mother was led into an office to sign some papers, Ashley wandered off to see what she could of the hospital. She stepped into a wide corridor and pulled up shortly when a man, warbling like a bird, almost bounced into her.

"Get me my shoes!" he commanded Ashley. "I am going down to the office, get me my shoes." He pointed in the direction of the nurses' station. He was middle-aged with graying temples and hairline. His eyes were large and seemed ready to pop out of their sockets.

Ashley backed away in silent terror, looking around for help but there was no one on the corridor.

"Get me my shoes and bring my car keys too, I need to get to the office!" The voice had become several octaves higher and was teetering on a scream.

Immediately, there were the sound of running feet and shouts of "Henry! Henry! Come here this minute! Henry, how did you get down here?" Two huge men appeared and instantly grabbed him.

"You know you're not supposed to be down here," one of them scolded, but not too unkindly.

"He must have dodged out of the bathroom when Renae was talking to me," the other one commented.

"Is this a new patient?" the first one asked, looking suspiciously at Ashley.

"I am sure I look saner than you!" Ashley retorted, annoyed that she should be asked such a question.

"Sorry Miss, but we get new patients all the time, and anybody, anybody can be a patient!" He emphasized the 'anybody', and they both walked off with Henry between them, still asking for his shoes, even while he was being gently reprimanded.

Ashley recovered quickly and continued her walk, but this time she kept a wary eye out for any other patients on the loose. She noticed that most of the interior was painted with soft shades, and that the walls were very clean. The wide corridor opened into a very large room, and Ashley saw a number of people in it. It seemed to be a common room or the area designated for the patients to gather. There were long leather settees, and dining chairs and tables. There was a  large television set at the front and some of the patients were huddled in small groups, watching the antics of two dancers, dancing to dancehall music. "Watch yuh back, when you gout pan di road," the voice warned and the dancers enacted the warning by sketching dance moves while looking furtively over their shoulders. Some of the patients laughed uproariously and one got up, stood in front of the television and shouted to it, "Shut up idiot, gwaan a yuh bed!"

A tall, heavyset man appeared beside him and took him back to his seat.

"Why you don't leave him alone?" one of the patients shouted at the man. "Him are to do what him mother tell him to do. You give yourself too much trouble! You go, go sit an' behave you little self, rude!" The man, who Ashley later learnt was a psychiatric attendant, did not respond but went and sat in his former seat.

She looked around and noticed others dressed in a similar manner seated among the patients and at strategic points around the room. There were also nurses, some in white and blue, also seated among them. A few of the nurses and psychiatric attendants were conversing with some of those who were not watching television. Ashley noticed that they were also playing cards and board games. A few of the patients were reading their Bibles and other books. One shouted out "Amen", jumped up from his seat and held his open Bible to the ceiling.

Ashley's heart went out to the patients. She wished that there was something she could do for them, something she could do for her sister who was in an even worse condition. She felt a touch on her shoulder and looked up into the face of a security guard who told her softly but firmly that it was not visiting hours so she should not be standing at the doorway and peeping in. At the same time, her phone rang and her anxious mother told her that she was waiting by the security post.

Ashley hurried to her mother and they left the hospital and drove home in silence. Their grief was too fresh, too undefined, too difficult to come to terms with. They both cried themselves to sleep that night.

In the subsequent weeks, Deidre-Ann seemed to grow worse. Her body was healing but her mind had an agenda of its own. It was still a constant struggle for the doctors to do their job. She kicked and hit at them telling them to go and wash their dirty hands. There was one particular nurse that she liked, Nurse Solomon, who could get her to do almost anything. She was the only one who could read to her and encourage her to take her medication.

On the days when she was really bad, she would scream and fight with herself. She constantly told phantoms to let her go and take their dirty hands off her. She would walk around her room warding off unseen persons. Mrs. Lenworth, after witnessing the same pattern of behavior for a while, decided that it had something to do with the night she was raped. She must have tried to ward off her attacker, and she imagined her putting up a good fight. When she got too boisterous, she had to be sedated. Mrs. Lenworth hated the injections. They not only robbed her of her humanity but rendered her almost lifeless. At times she would just lay in her bed looking at the ceiling as if she were having a silent conversation with someone up there and was really listening intently. She would sometimes nod and point to the unseen persons.

The hospital had a number of activities designed for socialization and as a way to draw the patients out of themselves. Deidre-Ann did not participate, she just sat and stared at the others, sometimes smiling and sometimes sleeping. Occassionally, the ones who were mending satisfactorily and were controllable would be taken outside for games, to sit in the garden and be read to, or just to walk around and enjoy the scenery. Deidre-Ann was taken out only once as she was deemed not ready to go out as yet.

Each patient was also assigned a psychiatrist, someone they could talk to, who would try to get to the cause or root of the illness and make recommendations. Deidre-Ann's psychiatrist did not get very far with her. The police had hoped that during these talks she would consciously reveal something about the rapist, but the physical blows and the emotional trauma seemed to have erased the incident from her mind. She didn't remember anything about home or school or the incident. Everyone was disappointed.

It was the holiday period so Ashley was able to accompany her mother on the daily evening visits. Other family members also gave their support and on an average evening she had no fewer than four visitors. For Mrs. Lenworth and Ashley, visiting the hospital did not just mean going to see Deidre-Ann alone. While someone was always with Deidre-Ann, they also found a little time to visit with some of the other patients and learn their story, sometimes from other visitors and sometimes from the patients themselves. They made the startling discovery that unlike the perception of many, one did not have to be insane to require psychiatric help. Some of the patients were simply undergoing stress or were deeply depressed. There were at least three patients that they could not determine whether anything was mentally wrong with them. They reasoned quite intelligently and talked about their lives with clarity. For two of them, they later learnt that their families had abandoned them and though they were well enough to go home, just did not have anyone to care for them. It was really touching.

Ashley found that for someone who formerly did not really care about people and their problems, she was giving more than a listening ear. She even took it on herself to make contact with the relatives of one of those who had been abandoned and was very close to persuading them to take back the patient into normal society. Ashley was also shocked to realize that mental illness could happen just like physical illness, and that no class, race, religion, age, or creed, were exempt. She had questioned how something like this could have happened to Deidre-Ann but she gained a little more understanding when she saw the politician's son, the university student, the bishop's daughter, the highly successful businessman whom illness had levelled with the so-called ordinary vendor, the singer, drug addict, domestic worker and handy-man. For the first time she fully understood the poem "Death the Leveller". The lines clanged disturbingly in her ears.

One evening, five weeks later, they arrived at the hospital after a very trying day. Mrs. Lenworth had to double up on work she had neglected since her daughter's ordeal and Ashley felt exceedingly tired as a result of the daily visits and sleeping fitfully at nights. Mrs. Lenworth was glad at first when Marla and her mother said they would visit that evening. She felt she would stay home and get some early sleep, but when Ashley arrived at her work place, she felt compelled to go to the hospital.

When they arrived, there were the medical officials, psychiatric attendants and some of the security guards all over the place. The Lenworth's heart quickened with anxiety as they cleared security. The guards looked at them unusually long and Mrs. Lenworth looked questioningly at Ashley. As they made their way to Deidre-Ann's room, a nurse blocked their way.

"Mrs. Lenworth, Ashley, there's a slight problem." She looked from one to the other, embarrassed.

"What is it nurse? Something seems to be wrong." Ashley felt her heart thumping furiously against her chest.

The nurse looked away from them and stared at the wall in front of her. "You see, we cannot find Deidre-Ann." It was a statement she had difficulty uttering.

"Find! What do you mean can't find?" Ashley grabbed the nurse's hand in panic.

"You are not talking about my daughter, are you nurse!" Mrs. Lenworth moved towards the nurse, her eyes and her mouth gawking.

"It's difficult to explain, but one minute she was in her room and then when the nurse went in with her medication she was gone, disappeared, vanished!" She looked worriedly from one to the other, searching for understanding. She found none.

"Nurse, she was left in your care, so you had better find her and find her quick!" The nurse moved off and left the Lenworths standing in consternation.

Ashley was the first to speak. "Mummy, we cannot just stand here, we need to help them look."

Mrs. Lenworth jerked into action. She nodded and followed her daughter. A thought struck her as she walked hurriedly along. "But Ash, they know this place better than we do. Where do you think we can possibly look that they haven't looked?"

Ashley looked at her and nodded in agreement but continued to walk. "We cannot just stand here and do nothing, we have to walk around."

"But how could she have got pass the security at the gate? They are always there," Mrs. Lenworth reasoned. "In addition, unless she somehow found the strength to remove a number of louvers, she would not be able to get outside."

"That's true and unless she slipped out unseen behind somebody, she should be still in the building. I wonder if she wandered over to the male section?" Ashley mused.

"I don't think so because they are very strict about that kind of thing. Something very bad happened one time that almost got them into trouble."

"We will still walk around and look. It's better than just standing here doing nothing." She was frantic with anxiety and fear.

They walked around for a while but it was more like getting into the searchers' way. Everyone was trying to avoid them and kept answering evasively when questioned. Ashley and Mrs. Lenworth went outside and sat on one of the stone benches. They did not speak to each other, as each was trying to work out Deidre-Ann's mysterious disappearance. Ashley reasoned that unless someone had aided her in getting away, she was right there on the compound. But what if she had got away by herself, where would she be now? She was in no condition to take care of herself, and there were no ends of evil men wait-ing out there to pounce on those who were not able to take care of themselves, men like those who had hurt her in the first instance. Ashley felt she could no longer sit down while her sister was in danger, so she got up and told her mother to follow her inside Deidre-Ann's room.

Mrs. Lenworth followed without a word. She felt as if her blood pressure was soaring towards the sky and that there was nothing she could do to control it. Ashley could not explain why she went back to Deidre-Ann's room and insisted that she wanted to sit in it for a while despite the nurse's disapproval that she could not.

"Find her and then chase me out!" Ashley retorted angrily. "You better find her and quickly before I call the police!" Her frustration and fear caused her to lash out.

"Well, Miss, we are doing the best we can!" the nurse fired back, annoyed at being ticked off.

"You had better do it quickly before we call in the police," a worried looking Mrs. Lenworth added.

The nurse glared at her and walked off, throwing up her hands and petitioning the air.

The Lenworths went back to Deidre-Ann's room. Mrs. Lenworth sat on the chair with her head in her hands while Ashley examined the contents on top of the chest of drawers. A plastic comb slipped from her hand and landed at the bedside closer to the wall. Ashley followed it with her eyes and decided to leave it there, but changed her mind.

As she bent down to pick up the comb, she realized that a part of it had gone under the bed. When she pushed her hand under the bed, she pulled it back suddenly as if something had stung her. She gave a little cry and stepped back.

Her mother jumped up at the sound. "Ash what's the matter? Ash what is wrong?"

"I...I felt something under the bed!" Ashley spoke almost in a whisper.

"What do you mean, feel something under the bed?" Mrs. Lenworth asked, moving around to the side of the bed. Forgetting her headache, she bent down and then she knelt and gave a scream. Ashley rushed to her side and then she too started screaming. Footsteps and shouts could be heard coming towards them.

"What is it? What is it?" a surprised voice asked. "What is the screaming about?"

"There, under there!" Ashley said, backing away from the bed. "Someone is under there and there is no sound or movement!"

"Somebody! Where? God have mercy!" came another awed voice.

"Over here! Are you deaf?" Mrs. Lenworth cried, pointing towards the bed.

A small group rushed towards the bedside even as the Lenworths backed away frightened and weakened by fear.

"Oh God, it's the girl!" another voice reported.

"Let us lift her up and put her on the bed!" someone suggested.

"Is she dead?" someone asked in a hushed tone.

"Call the doctor quickly somebody!" another voice commanded.

"Jesus, it's Ann," Mrs. Lenworth said and slumped to the floor.

For a while Ashley stood, fear nailing her to the spot, her adrenaline refusing to support her, then as if pushed from behind, she rushed to her mother. "Help her quickly! Please help her! Somebody help her!"

For a while, confusion mastered the moment, then two doctors arrived and started giving orders. "Place the lady on the empty bed next door. Nurse Simpson, you go with Doctor Raine. Nurse Daley, you stay with me and everyone else go back to your station!"

Ashley watched numbed, yet spell bound as the room emptied around them. Everyone wanted to stay, but no one dared disobey the doctor's strict order. He looked around, saw Ashley and asked, "Are they your relatives?"

"Yes, my sister and my mother." The words forced themselves unwillingly from her mouth as she looked at her sister on the bed and noticed for the first time what seemed like a piece of cloth wrapped around her neck. She almost cried out but managed to smother it.

The doctor followed her gaze and then turned to the nurse. "Nurse take her to the nurses' station and let her stay there, then ask another nurse to come back with you." His voice sounded hard and firm but there was a chord of sympathy in it.

Ashley allowed herself to be ushered out of the room. Thorns of pain pricked her head mercilessly and she was glad to be given a seat in the nurses' station. She held her head in her hands and could not stop the groan which escaped.

"Are you alright?" An anxious nurse hovered beside her.

"No," said Ashley. "My head is going to explode this minute."

A nurse rushed forward with two painkillers. "Take these and then come and lie on the bed in the little room."

Gratefully, Ashley swallowed the pills and again allowed herself to be guided. She sank into the small bed and in a few minutes she was as dead to the world as her mother and sister.

# CHAPTER FIVE

## *Deidre-Ann Returns To Her Senses*

*A*shley jumped up and almost fell out of the bed. She tried to adjust her eyes to the semi-darkness which had crept into the room. For a while, she struggled to remember where she was and how she had got there, and even what day it was. Then like a sudden flash of lightning it hit her. She pushed her feet into her slippers and suddenly dashed into the nurses' station, rubbing her eyes and trying to ignore the dull throb that was rhythmically playing at the sides and back of her head. She started rushing towards Deidre-Ann's room but the nurses stopped her.

"The doctor is still with her, you can't go in there just yet."

"I want to see my mother in the meantime," she informed the nurse. They did not stop her so she went into the room. Her mother was sitting in a chair looking pale and confused. She jumped up when Ashley burst into the room.

"Mummy, you really have to stop fainting so much." Ashley greeted her with a hug.

"I thought I was a strong woman but these days I am getting weaker than the puniest child. These problems are more than I can bear." Her plaintive tone brought tears to her daughter's eyes.

"Mummy, you are no less human than the rest of us. Each person bears grief in his own way. There are some who show no signs outside but inside is all shattered and shredded, and if it continues too long, psychological problems result. Then there are those who crumble outwardly but are somehow healed by tears and support from others, and there are those who mourn in ways which I cannot explain, only God knows."

"You put me to shame girl, for a while you sounded so old and wise; telling me what I should be telling you." She hugged her daughter closely, reaching out for strength and support. "I wonder how Ann got under that bed," she remarked, voicing the subject bombarding her mind.

"They will have to explain that and the clothes around her neck," Ashley said, her heart falling sickly into the pit of her stomach.

"Clothes around her neck!" Mrs. Lenworth exclaimed, breaking free from Ashley. "Clothes around her neck! What are you talking about?" The fright and confusion had seeped back into her voice.

Ashley sat down on the bed and looked down at the floor as if she was seeking aid from it. "Mummy, Ann had something around her neck." She rose her head slowly and met her mother's gaze. "Mummy, I think she was trying to kill herself." Having voiced the unthinkable, she gazed away from her mother into vacant nothingness.

Mrs. Lenworth did not reply. Knowing the type of personality that Deidre-Ann had, she thought she would have rallied back quickly, fighting the pain and shame and flouting the odds. Deidre-Ann had always been someone to forget a problem easily and move on, someone whose philosophy was live and let live, someone whose attitude was tomorrow would work itself out. One never knew how he or she would deal with a problem unless that person finds him or herself immersed in the same muddy water and tried to keep afloat. When Deidre-Ann came back to herself fully she hoped her philosophy of life would have changed.

"I am going to find the doctor whether he's ready for me or not," Ashley said, jumping up. "These people have some explaining to do and I need answers now!"

Mrs. Lenworth fell in behind her and together they walked to Deidre-Ann's room. The doctor was still inside. Ashley knocked determinedly and prepared for an argument, deciding to stand her ground.

The doctor opened the door. He looked from one to the other and then told them to step inside. Deidre-Ann was lying on the bed, breathing easily and evenly. The Lenworths felt their hearts fighting to get back into their original place. The doctor looked at them, relaxed and ready to talk. "She is alright now, you don't have to worry." He stopped for a while then went on. "No one knows how it happened but she tore a nightie in two and tied it tightly around her neck. Sometime during that activity she fell off the bed unconscious and somehow rolled under it."

"How long do you think it happened before we found her?" Mrs. Lenworth asked.

"I don't know," the nurse replied. "They last saw her about 4:00 p.m. when she was given her medication. At that time she was lying in bed."

"And we found her about six," said Ashley. "Doctor, I think this is a case of negligence. It appears that once the patient seems to be asleep no one really pays them any attention!" Ashley could feel her short fuse getting ignited.

"How could you say that?" the doctor defended. "We do not have a record of negligence!" His voice held great surprise.

"Well, you have just established one!" Mrs. Lenworth said in a surly voice.

"This could have happened anywhere. It does not take more than a minute or two for what happened to have happened. I do not know any hospital where the patients are monitored every single minute." His tone was quiet but the hurt seeped through.

"In this type of institution, you need to watch every second." Ashley's voice rose to a dangerous pitch. "If it wasn't for chance we would not have found her until the cleaning lady was sweeping or something! You were negligent and we are not sure yet where this is going to end!"

"For God sakes, let it end here, please do not destroy the hospital. She is alive and will pull through. In addition, I am certain you do not want adverse publicity for your daughter and your family." His voice was calm but pleading. Ashley looked at him and felt her anger subsiding. He was a young man, maybe about thirty years old and she could imagine the dreams and plans he had for the future. Even though he had not been the doctor on call at the time, he was connected to the hospital and would still be hurt by the negative publicity. He had worked hard to save her sister's life and she thanked him for that beyond measure. She also reasoned that what he said about Ann not taking more than a minute or two to try and commit suicide was true. They could not have envisaged that anything like that was going to happen.

"Well, we will see what comes out of this," Ashley answered, turning away to stand by her sister's bed. She looked at the still figure and wondered how things could have gone so wrong. Why had life thrown them so much sudden misfortune? No one had ever dreamt in the remotest corner of his or her mind that this could ever happen, maybe to someone else but not to them. The saying "Trouble never set like rain" was certainly apt. She also thought it would be appropriate to add "Trouble zooms in like lightning, sudden and dangerous."

The two descriptions of trouble became even more fitting when she reached home that night and decided to check her grades for the semester. She had B+s and As for four courses and an E for one course. That examination had been done after her sister's ordeal started. She had never failed an examination at the university before and the shock of it hit her. The headache she had felt earlier at the hospital came back instantly, knife points of pain stabbed at her head and nape, and she rested her head on the computer. Her whole life was disintegrating around her and she had hardly heard from her friend since the family's problem. He was too busy to stand by her. Every time she called, she got his voice mail or the phone rang without an answer. Well it was good that she found out about him before she had really become too serious. 'A friend in need is a friend indeed' was certainly not his motto.

She did not want to add to her mother's worries so she did not tell her about her failure. She quickly turned off the computer and went towards the bedroom. She was halted by a weak squawk. She turned and went back into the washroom to look at Deidre-Ann's parrot. It was standing dispiritedly on its perch. It barely moved when Ashley pushed her finger through the mesh and touched it. "Hey Talk Waves, what's up? You don't talk anymore. Don't you know you are supposed to cheer up this family? Where's your voice?"

The bird hung his head slowly to one side and made a feeble sound. Ashley put some food into the cage, poured some water into a container and left. She really did not have the time or the urge to really clean out the cage as she should.

As she turned to go into her room the telephone rang. "I'll get it!" she shouted, not wanting her mother to answer it. She stood before it and waited until it stopped ringing. She was about to turn away when it started ringing again. She waited until it was at the last ring and then she picked up the telephone hesitantly, hands shaking. "What do you want now?" she hissed into the phone.

"You start get rude now my girl." A high-pitched squeaky voice laughed in an unnatural manner. "Just a reminder, don't try find out nothing 'bout yuh sister problem. She get deal with like she deserve, an' yuh next if the police continue!" The voice gave an unnerving laugh and then hung up.

Ashley stood where she was for a long while; she might have grown out of the ground, she was so still. That was the third call she had received from Mr. Anonymous. He kept changing his voice, one time it was mouse-like, another time it sounded like a Sunday school teacher, pleading and pious; and the first time it was gruff and grating. Ashley had not told her mother because she knew the panic and fear that would result. She could not bear the thought of her mother suffering any more. She would tell Nathan what was happening because at least one other person needed to know and who better than a family member who was already working on the case. She would warn him not to say a word to her mother.

She went to bed with her mind whirling like a ballet dancer doing a pirouette. It seemed to her like the un-leashed family misfortune was not about to just end with a single incident, but would go on indefinitely. Who could be calling to threaten them? She reasoned that Deidre-Ann had given her number to some of her friends because they often times called her. Who knew who the rapist was? It could very well be one of her male friends.

The following day, she went to see Nathan and told him about the threatening anonymous calls. Nathan was taken aback.

"So you have now become a target!" He looked at her bewildered. "Seems like we are dealing with some really serious criminals. They're not content to destroy one life, they want to destroy a whole family. Now Ash, you know that you have to be extra careful. You don't walk to any-where really but you never know. The university campus is big and all kinds of people find their way in. You really never know. When you go back to school if you ever find that you have problem to get home, call me right away. As a matter of fact, there is a colleague who works with the campus police that I will contact. In the mean time don't say anything at all to your mother and I'll find out how to get the house number changed at once. We don't have to worry about Ann's cell number because the criminal dem t'ief that phone. We never found it at all." He rested his chin on his hand as his thoughts absorbed him.

A few days later, after three more threatening telephone calls, Nathan convinced Mrs. Lenworth to change the number. He explained to her that it was just a safety precaution and that he knew a situation where some-thing untoward had happened with threatening phone calls. He convinced her that that was the last thing he wanted them to experience. He encouraged her to make arrangements for an unlisted number, and warned her not

to give the new number to all and sundry, especially to anyone from Deidre-Ann's school. She complied to all his
instructions and so the threatening calls at the home
stopped.

A month passed and Ashley returned to university.
Gerard presented himself with all manner of concocted
excuses but Ashley brushed him away, pointing out that it
was divine intervention that God had found a way to show
her what substance he was made of before the relationship became too serious. After a few futile attempts,
Gerard slinked away like an embarrassed dog with its
tail between its legs. When his friends inquired about
the demise of the relationship, he told them that Ashley
had too many sick family problems and he could not
handle them along with his studies.

Ashley's schedule was an extremely busy one and
with her full timetable and research and assignments to
be done, she could only visit her sister once per week and
on weekends. Her mother continued her unflagging daily
visits, refusing suggestions that she could sometimes miss
a day. Ashley had no idea how she managed at work. If this
tragic occurrence had not taken place, her mother would
not have discovered her resilience and determination.

The only beam of hope was the joyful news that after
five months, Deidre-Ann was improving. She actually
recognized her mother, Ashley, other family members
and Marla. She wanted to know why and when she had
been taken to the hospital. Ashley and Mrs. Lenworth did
not quite know how to explain the truth, not wanting to

hurt her all over and maybe send her reeling back into a relapse.

Ashley told her that she had an accident and had to be taken to the hospital. "Where did I hurt?" she wanted to know.

"You hurt your head badly and...and your legs!" Mrs. Lenworth looked away, trying not to meet her daughter's questioning eyes.

"My legs, what happened to my legs? I was not wearing a cast, was I? What did I break?" She looked surprisingly down at her legs and then looked back at her mother and sister.

Ashley felt like a cornered prey. How was she to explain to Deidre-Ann without actually mentioning the word rape?

While she was groping for words, her mother cleared her throat. "It was not your lower leg, it was more in the thigh area but don't worry, the doctor's fixed all that and there is no more pain. Soon you will be ready to go home."

She laughed and hugged her daughter, but Deidre-Ann did not hug her back.

"Mummy what's wrong with my head, you said my head is sick?" She felt all around her head as if she was trying to locate some kind of cut or bruise.

Ashley wished she knew how to explain that her head was sick in more ways than one. People who were having mental problems were usually in denial and that further compounded the problem, because how do you try to get well, if you're already well? Mrs. Lenworth looked at Ashley and her eyes said, *You take this one.*

While Deidre-Ann's eyes drilled steadily into Ashley's, Ashley rummaged through her brain for another answer. "You...you were hit in the head by a blunt instrument. We are not certain what it was so your head hurt you a lot and caused you to lose consciousness for a long time." Ashley spoke the words hurriedly as if she had been burnt and had to get rid of the substance, which was searing her tongue.

"How long have I been in the hospital?" Deidre-Ann asked, getting up from the bed and walking around the room.

Her mother and sister watched her. They were assessing her movements to see whether they were steady or erratic.

"Ash, when my head was hurting, did I behave like Tyrone?" She sat down on the bed again, a worried look clouding her face.

Tyrone was a teenage boy whom the doctors had diagnosed as having severe depression arising from a dysfunctional family. His mother had deserted her four children, Tyrone included, and had gone to the United States of America. Tyrone was five at the time and loved his mother dearly. As the years passed, he became withdrawn and deeply intense. He saw all females as potential mothers and became fixated on them. At the moment, he followed Miss Learne and Mrs. Deane around, cautioning them to go home and look after their children, and pointing out inadequacies in their housekeeping and child rearing as he saw fit.

"Don't you hear the baby crying?" he would shout loudly. "Why are you going away when the child is hungry?" Or "Mummy, that dinner is not cooked properly, it tastes like paper!"

Ashley did not answer, she just shook her head. Deidre-Ann did not ask any more questions that day.

Two weeks later, her memory surged back, like someone who had, like the fairy tale Rip Van Winkle, awakened from long years of deep sleep. The only difference was that she was the only one who had changed and not society or the people. It was Saturday and she was sitting outside on a stone bench, enjoying the cool whispering wind and the engaging scenery created by the trees, plants, flowers and grass. They were having a conversation about which fruits were her favourite, when she said without warning, "Mummy, Ash, I know I was raped."

Mrs. Lenworth almost fell from the bench. She quickly regained her balance and looked enquiringly at Ashley and then at Deidre-Ann. Deidre-Ann did not look at them but stared straight ahead. Her face was blank and expressionless, her eyes unblinking. Mrs. Lenworth moved over to her and hugged her closely. She could feel her heart pumping furiously against hers, but she didn't make a sound. There were no tears wetting her shoulders and no hysterical sobbing.

Mrs. Lenworth released her and looked at her, disbelief etched in her face. "Ann." She said her name softly almost sacredly, not wanting to hurt her in any way. "Ann, are you certain that you want to talk about this?"

"Well, there is nothing to talk about because that night is almost a blank. I only remember the ugly part and the pain, nothing else."

"But Ann, don't you have any idea who might have done this to you?" Ashley asked quietly, coaxingly, hoping to awaken her memory from the long sleep.

"No Ash, I don't and I don't even want to try. One day it will all come back and then I will have to deal with it." She fell silent and stared off into nothingness, the vacant look on her face telling them that the matter had been suspended for the time being and that no amount of coaxing and cajoling would budge her.

Ashley was happy at the turn of events and she knew her sister was ready to come home, but there was one frightening thought which had been her constant companion since the calls had started. Deidre-Ann would always be in danger because once her assailant or assailants knew that she was out, he or they would want to harm her to protect himself or themselves. Without warning, a finger of pain poked her at the back of her head and she winced.

It seemed as though their problems were only just beginning.

# CHAPTER SIX

## Home And Then To School

*D*eidre-Ann held her folder protectively in front of her. Her purple and white bag was secure on her back as she walked into the classroom. She kept her head down and made her way to the extreme back of the classroom and sat down in what she hoped was out of sight and scrutiny of both teachers and students. She still held her folder in her hand and her bag was still anchored firmly to her back.

She looked around timidly as a mongoose, who was trying to see if the coast was clear before dashing across the road to hide itself in the bushes. The students trickled in slowly at first and then a large number of them came just before the bell. They were laughing and talking loudly, filled with exuberance and seemed too carefree. They reminded Deidre-Ann of birds squawking and moving around aimlessly, their voices distended and unrestrained. Deidre-Ann wished she could share their vivacity, but her heartbeat had accelerated and was fisting her chest painfully. She did not feel comfortable and wanted to go home, where she could go unnoticed, undetected, unobstructed. She was afraid to lift her eyes because even though she was not in her old school and even though this was more than a year later than her ordeal, she had no way of knowing whether anyone would identify her and then the gossip would start and the sickness would come back. Some students glanced at her curiously as she sat there with her head bent, poring over her now opened folder. They wondered who this new studious girl was; school had not even started and there she was quite absorbed in her work.

The neatly arranged processed hair which caressed her shoulders drew two students to her seat. The young man cleared his throat to signal his presence and said, "Hi, are you new?"

Deidre-Ann recoiled, her first instinct was to get up and run. She could feel hysteria beginning to set in. She kept her head down and mumbled, "Yes."

"My name is Kanique, what's yours?"

"Deidre-Ann," she muttered, again without even an upward glance.

Kanique took the message from the almost monosyllabic answer and moved off. "See you around Deidre-Ann."

"What a strange girl," he remarked to his male companion. "Except for the hair, I didn't get a good look at her; she wouldn't even lift her head."

"Kan, that's how new students behave sometimes. They don't know anyone so they are shy and behave as if they can't talk," the young man said, defending Deidre-Ann.

"I hope you're right because if she is going to be in our class, she has to be sociable," Kanique replied.

The clanging bell intruded into Deidre-Ann's thoughts. This was one of the moments she dreaded, general assembly. Now everyone would stare at her and ask questions. She hoped they would ask them of other people and not of her. Her bag was still on her back and she still clutched her folder as if it were a means of protection or solace. She stood at the back, not caring whether she was in the right line or not. She kept her head down and hardly listened. She did not participate in the singing and only mouthed the 'Our Father' prayer. Her aim was to be as inconspicuous as possible.

The day passed uneventfully, except for her standing in class and giving her name. She sat at the back of the class as she had in the morning and did not speak unless directly spoken to. It was close to dismissal that she overheard the conversation. A group of students were gossiping just outside her classroom window. She did not pay much attention to them until she heard her name.

"That new girl, the one who sat at the back is very pretty," the first voice remarked.

"Yes, but she seems to be withdrawn and a little strange, don't you think?" the second replied.

"She seems to be a bit on the older side," another remarked.

"Yes," chipped in another voice. "She doesn't seem to be in our age group. She looks about two years older than us. Ah wonder..." her voice trailed off, its puzzled tone filled with supposition.

"I don't know if you're thinking what I'm thinking, but ah wonder if she is one of those girls that the Women's Centre transfer from one school to another?" The voice held suspicion and a hint of excitement.

"You mean maybe she is a teenage mother. She probably have a baby and since they don't recommend that they go back to the same old school because of how children normally treat them, they send them elsewhere," the first voice furnished with a knowledgeable 'that must be it' tone.

"That is possible, yuh memba Lorna Fayne last year?" a male voice joined in the search for answers.

"Yes, but she neva last. She couldn't tek the wickedness that the students dish out to her," a sympathetic voice said.

"Ah don't see why people have to behave like that, cause sometimes is not really bad the girls bad, is just mistake dem make," the sympathetic voice continued. "Everybody entitled to dem one or two mistake and ah don't see why we have to treat them like they come from the fringes." Her criticism was tinged with annoyance as she alluded to the group of outcasts in a science fiction novel she had read.

"Well, I hope that don't happen to this girl. It would be too bad, she is such a pretty thing," the male voice chimed in again.

"Yes, you would have to notice that," a female teased. "Next thing you know, you run go talk to her." She elbowed him playfully.

The bell rang and they moved away, the discussion suspended for the time being. Deidre-Ann sat trance-like, rehashing the conversation in her mind. So that was what they thought of her. Well, it was better than actually knowing what had happened to her and where she had spent the most horrifying few months of her life. People attached a negative stigma to anyone who had been a patient of a mental institution. It was better to be labelled a teenage mother than a mental case. Let them keep their assumption, she would have to live with it.

She had never been so glad to see anyone in her life than she was to see her mother at the end of the day. She hastily jumped into the car and closed out the school. As she drove away, curious eyes followed her, noting the serious, relieved look on her face.

"How was your day?" her mother asked, reaching over and touching her face anxiously.

"Let's just say I survived," Deidre-Ann answered without furnishing any details.

"Come on Ann, you know I want to hear more than just that. Did you make any new friends? Tell me about it," she coaxed slowly, as if she were addressing a small child.

"New friends? Mom you know I would never bother with those things again! Friends are for when you are popular and when things are going well." Deidre-Ann's voice was cool and lifeless.

"Ann, I know how you feel. I am your mother I watched you suffer and I suffered along with you, but remember Marla never stopped being your friend."

"Marla is alright, but can you imagine what all the others said about me." She looked away from her mother and became engrossed in the scenery. She watched a flight of birds as they soared nonchalantly above the clouds singing heedlessly, flaunting their happiness to the world. She envisaged herself as a bird flying away from her glum world of sadness and despondency. She would fly across the ocean and then she would settle in a strange new land where she was unknown and where all her problems would go away.

"Ann! Ann!" Her mother was calling her, the anxiety which had become a part of her was evident in her voice. "Ann, remember the talk you had with the family last night. You promised to try and cope and if you can remember I am here for you and so are all the members of our family. Don't worry, it will all come right again. Everything will be fine."

Deidre-Ann listened to her half-heartedly. She sounded as though she was trying to convince herself. If everything was going to be fine, then why did she sound so disconsolate? And why was she, Deidre-Ann, feeling so apprehensive and jittery?

In the sanctuary of her room, she lay quietly and stared at the ceiling. She had taken her medication so she was feeling calm and focused. She forced her mind to go back to that fateful night but the details eluded her.

She recollected going in search of Mrs. Munroe who was supposed to be in the last classroom on the grade eleven block. She had wondered why Mrs. Munroe had chosen to speak to her in an area so far removed from everything. She had gone there only to find the classroom closed and the place in darkness. As she exclaimed and turned to retrace her steps, crude, strong hands grabbed her forcefully from behind and covered her mouth, trapping her scream. Her mind went empty at that point, but the scream which had been imprisoned for so long finally freed itself. It was long and guttural; a release from the caverns of the soul that sent shivers of fear into her mother and sister who came running. They got into the bed with her and held her tightly, reassuringly, as her heart pumped away, threatening to break free from its moor. Their whispered words of comfort did much to pacify her as quiet tears rolled unchecked, dampening her nightclothes.

Finally, she fell asleep, a fitful troubled sleep, where hands were grabbing at her and children wearing black and white uniforms were laughing and pointing at her, blocking her path as she ran this way and that, trying to escape. She awoke panting, but this time she suppressed the scream, not wanting to disturb her family and make them think that she was getting ill again. She had seen the concern on their faces earlier that evening.

At school that day, she seemed even more withdrawn. Any seemingly unusual glance from anyone sent her scurrying inwardly, locking in herself tighter than before.

At lunchtime she decided to eat the fruits she had taken with her instead of purchasing lunch at the cafeteria. While she was eating, she remembered that she had the money in her bag that she was supposed to take to two teachers for two text books. She finished her lunch and then started for the staffroom. She was almost at the door when she pulled up suddenly, a familiar voice had called out her name.

"Deidre-Ann what a surprise, I didn't know you were attending this school! When did you begin? I started on Monday."

Deidre-Ann stopped midway in her steps. She did not want to turn around so that Meichi Anderson could see the fright in her eyes. They were jumping uncontrollably, wanting to escape their sockets and leave her blind. Deidre-Ann thought that temporary blindness would be a good thing since it would prevent her from seeing Meichi's inquisitive face. She had been a part of her former cheerleading squad and was known for her prying, mischievous ways. It was she who had informed the school that Yvonne Jackson, a grade eleven student at the time, was living in a one-room house with her parents and other siblings.

Deidre-Ann tried to control her tremulous hands which seemed bent on throwing her folder to the ground. "Hi Meichi," she answered. "How are you?" She started to walk away but Meichi's voice stopped her.

"You still look good after that thing happen to you. Dem don't catch anybody yet?" As she spoke her eyes assessed Deidre-Ann from her face down to her shoes.

Deidre-Ann withstood the searching assessment without flinching outwardly. She then moved off without responding to Meichi. The nerves in her face were throbbing viciously in partnership with her leaping eyes.

"Deidre you can answer me, we used to have fun in cheerleading!" She started after her but thought better of it and halted. She watched her go, turning once to glance at her and this happened to be the very minute when a girl from her class who had been standing by the staffroom walked over to her.

Deidre-Ann knew what would happen from there and she knew what she had to do. She walked towards the gate and bided her time. As soon as the guard became engaged in talking to the driver of a van seeking permission to enter the school, she quickly let herself through the pedestrian gate and without once looking back, rounded the bend and disappeared down the road.

Mrs. Lenworth looked at her watch anxiously and wondered what could be keeping Deidre-Ann. She had been waiting for her for more than twenty minutes. She could not really ask any of the students for her because she knew that this was her second day and not many students would know her. She watched them as they laughed and talked together, sometimes playfully hitting and hugging one another. They were like normal children ought to be and she wished that Deidre-Ann would get back to her former bubbly out-going self. She had been through enough for a young girl, enough to last her for a lifetime and beyond. She needed a large dose of happiness, not the transient one that disappeared after one gulp, but something that could be sustained, something lasting that could be savoured. She shook her head, realizing that life was not that way, no huge chunks of happiness, just snatches that you were privileged to sample, some sampling a little more than others.

Mrs. Lenworth shook herself out of her reverie and decided to go in search of her daughter. She did not ask for her but simply walked and looked among the students. The feeling of déjà vu was returning and with it, fresh panic. She made her way to the front desk and asked the secretary if she could get the administration to make an announcement asking Deidre-Ann Lenworth to meet her at the front desk.

The vice principal complied, but no Deidre-Ann came. Mrs. Lenworth called Nathan. As she waited for him to come, she felt a constriction in her heart. She felt as if someone was tugging at the strings in an effort to remove it. She willed herself to keep calm and whispered fiercely to herself that she would not panic because it was a fact that lightning did not strike in the same place twice. Deidre-Ann might not be around but it could not be that it was the same experience again, maybe she was just tired and had fallen asleep somewhere. Since she had been to the hospital she had lost her usual vivacity and only did something because she had to. She no longer wanted to dress up in new outfits and had secretly thrown away some of the fancy ones. Her mother had found them only a week before in a bag when she was throwing out the garbage. She had taken out the bag and hidden it in the garage without saying a word to Deidre-Ann or her sister. Her motivation for most things had waned. She hardly threw a cursory glance at the parrot, Talk Waves. The lethargic bird had rushed back to life when Deidre-Ann came home, but apart from feeding it sometimes, she hardly looked at it. The bird, sensing her dejection, had returned to its former feebleness, barely squawking or talking. It too had lost its salt. It was as if its tongue had been removed.

When Nathan came, he looked at her anxiously. Her face was a strange red and her eyes had a trance-like look with disbelief carved in them. Nathan held her and felt the quiver rippling through her body.

"Don't worry." He tried to sound as gentle as he could. "She can't be very far away. She must be somewhere around, maybe talking to a teacher about a course or something." His voice was reassuring but when he let her go and she looked into his eyes, there was a suggestion of fear, a look of 'this can't be happening again'. "Let us walk around and look," he suggested, "and if we don't see her, we must speak to the principal."

A walk around yielded nothing, so Nathan went to the principal's office to speak with him. He had not seen Deidre-Ann since school started so he had not got a chance to find out how she was settling in. He went to the intercom and asked the students from her class who were still on the compound to report to his office. Three students came forward and after being questioned, they revealed that she had not been back to class after lunch. One of them also told him that a man had been asking for her earlier.

"A man!" Nathan blurted out in surprise.

"Yes, he was asking if she had gone home yet. He said he was her father," the student reported.

"Her father," Mrs. Lenworth interjected. "What does he look like?"

"He was short, not really that dark and not really that slim with a moustache and graying beard."

"That is not her father," Nathan said forcefully.

"Definitely not," agreed Mrs. Lenworth. "I wonder what that person wanted?"

"He said he had come to pick her up," the student offered. "He even walked around for a while looking for her."

"Did he leave with anyone?" The principal asked anxiously.

"I don't know Sir, because he was walking all around and we did not follow him. We thought he was really her father," the student replied.

"Do you know if anyone told him that she did not go to class since lunch?" Nathan asked, looking at the student searchingly.

"I don't think so Sir. Unless we really have something against somebody and really want them to get punishment, we wouldn't really do that," another student volunteered.

They left the school after searching the grounds and calling Ashley. They drove out most of the area around the school and having no success, they started combing the city. While they drove, Nathan sought clarity on some issues related to Deidre-Ann.

"Carm, whose idea was it to send Deidre-Ann back to school so quickly?"

"Well, she had already missed over a year and since she wasn't sick anymore, we decided it was time for her to get back into the real world and try and pick up where she left off," Mrs. Lenworth said defensively.

"But what did Ann think about this, I mean, did she really want to go back to school?"

"To tell the truth, she didn't really want to leave the house for anything at all. She felt that she could manage the exam on her own and wanted me to enter her as a private candidate," Mrs. Lenworth told Nathan.

"But why couldn't that plan work?" Nathan wanted to know. "She was almost ready for her exam when her ordeal happened. All she had to do was revise, you know she is a bright girl."

"I honestly don't think that would have worked after so long and more over, she had to face the real world sometime or the other, and staying at home indefinitely would not have been the answer." Mrs. Lenworth defended herself stoutly.

"But Carm, couldn't you have given her more time. I definitely don't think she was ready to mix with people!" Nathan persisted.

"You might not agree with me but I was doing what I thought was best for her. Someone has to help her get back into the world." A dubious note had crept into her voice. She didn't seem so certain about her decision anymore.

Nathan felt sorry for her and decided to talk about something else so he turned the topic to the strange visitor. "Does he sound like anybody you have ever seen before?"

"No and even if Jeffrey has changed himself some-how, he couldn't alter his height. You don't change from tall to medium height just by thinking about it!"

"And Jeffrey is a brown man, unless he had tanned himself black." She tried to laugh along with Nathan, but the laughter petered off as the seriousness of the situation slapped her in the face. "What are we going to do Nathan, are we going to report her as being missing?"

"I don't think we should do that so quickly because her picture flashed around the country and the internet would only create more danger from whoever is looking for her." He obviously had thought out the situation.

"I will go along with you on this one for the time being, but if we don't find her soon, we have to publicize it." Her voice was fearful and Nathan knew that she was undergoing more pain and stress than ever, and she would have to be careful or else she would wind up in the same place Ann was coming from.

An overwrought Ashley was able to provide a little light on the strange man who had gone asking for Deidre-Ann. "I have seen that man before," she revealed after hearing the description. "He visited the hospital a few times when Ann was there."

"What do you mean visited the hospital?" her mother asked.

"I don't know who he was supposed to be visiting but I know I saw him a few times going in and out of the hospital. Whenever my eyes met his, he would glance away quickly and hold down his head as if he was hiding something. He acted strange. I wonder how he knew Ann was going to a new school and why was he posing as her father?" Her face wore a look of consternation.

"But how come you never mention him before?" Nathan enquired.

"I didn't give much thought about him. He was just another strange person in a place where one would expect strangeness. But how come he knew that Ann was going to that school? It is a new school and except for our family, we did not discuss our plans with anyone!" She stared past her mother and cousin and focused her eyes on nothingness. The threatening calls that still came in even after the telephone number had been changed, loomed large in her mind. She had not told her mother about them even when she had remarked that sometimes when the phone rang and she answered it, all she could hear was heavy breathing. The person always reserved the messages for Ashley who never delivered them. Deidre-Ann never answered the telephone even if she was alone at home.

She seemed to have developed an aversion for the phone. She never called anyone. They had to force her to take one to school and told her to answer only if the numbers were theirs. Now she was not answering at all and her family was where they had been that fateful night, more than a year before; the only difference was then, they had a battered body, now they had none.

# CHAPTER SEVEN

# Deidre-Ann On The Street

The bus stopped and Deidre-Ann looked around her. The bus was emptying around her but she made no move to get off. She watched as if from afar off. It was as though she was a bystander and not one of the passengers.

After everyone was gone she still sat, a stone could not have been more immobile, more fixed. She had no plans and did not know where she was going, but she knew she was not going back home, at least not yet, not until she had found a way to convince her mother not to send her back to school, but to let her stay at home and work; home where she did not have to meet prying, probing humans who wanted to invade her space and pretend to be friends when they thought she was popular, but would cast accusing, hypocritical condemning eyes on her when they found out what human scum had stolen from her. She didn't want to be a part of their society anymore. The only trouble was everywhere one turned, the scum were present in every guise, age and stage, smiling, frowning, wheedling, threatening. She wondered how she could ever find a railroad to freedom, freedom to isolation, freedom to independence, freedom and peace from humanity.

"Miss, unless you want to go back to where you are coming from, you have to get off the bus now!" a voice shouted at her. She looked up and saw the bus driver coming towards her. His narrow, leathery face held an amused, questioning smile.

For a moment, Deidre-Ann just glared at him, but as he got closer, she recoiled and fearing this replica of humanity would encroach on her, she sprang up as if she had been bitten by a venomous viper and made her way hastily through the back door.

The driver looked at the fleeing girl and shook his head. "Poor pretty soul, she look really out of it. Ah wonder what is her problem?" he said softly to himself. He stepped out of the bus and tried to locate her, but she had merged with the rushing, scurrying crowd which was a consistent part of the city's terminus, especially on weekdays.

Deidre-Ann had never taken a bus before. She had no idea where each one went except when she read the rotating information at the front of each bus. She crossed the road from the terminus because so many people seemed to be crossing, but when she got to the other side of the road, she stood on the sidewalk, not knowing where to go or what to do. She stood at one place for about half an hour, just watching the city swirling around her. At intervals she looked at her watch, not because she necessarily wanted to see the time, because she was not going any-where in particular, but to give the impression that she was waiting for someone. She watched students talking animatedly to one another. Some of the older ones were in pairs and others seemed to be seeking partners. The older people did not dawdle, or engage in too much chatter, they walked purposefully by, seemingly bent on getting home or back to work. The white collar workers were a mixture of business and pleasure; some ladies' stilleto heels struck the asphalt savagely, threatening to create minute potholes, others strolled in a Sunday morning manner, stopping to examine the wares of the shouting venders and conversing comfortably with them.

Deidre-Ann watched it all, untouched by the activity. As she examined her watch another time, a voice nearby said to her, "Ah watching you a long time waiting on your boyfriend, you no see him stan' you up, come go with me instead."

Deidre-Ann looked up into the bearded smiling face of a young man. He was holding a cellular phone in one hand and an attaché case in the other. She moved away from him and followed the people as they crossed to the other side of the road. She looked back and saw the young man watching her from across the road. At the same time she, heard a taxi-driver shouting, "Peyton Gardens, Peyton Gardens, one and ready, comfortable car with AC leaving right now!"

She made her way towards the taxi and got in. She had been to Peyton Gardens with her mother several times when she was younger. She remembered having fun visiting the animals in their cages, mocking and making funny faces at them. She also remembered buying fruits, baked products, confectionery, ice-cream and other delicacies. At least this was one place she knew which had pleasant memories for her. She glanced furtively at the other passengers, but they seemed not to notice her, they were all wrapped up in their own world.

Everyone got off the taxi before Deidre-Ann. She was seated at the back and watched the driver carefully. She breathed gratefully when he turned in at Peyton Gate, allowed her to exit the vehicle and drove away without a word or backward glance.

Deidre-Ann made her way through the gate slowly. She was keeping an eye out for anyone that she might know. She had no idea what she was going to do, but knew she was not going home to be forced back into school. Without any doubt, she loved her mother and sister dearly and appreciated what they had done for her, but they had never been raped and could not fully empathize with her intense loathing of people, especially men. She would just ride aimlessly along with the tide and see where it dumped her.

She picked out a secluded area of the park and sat on the ground but no sooner had she taken a seat, than warning bells pealed in her head. Seclusion was not a safe way for her, even though it was still early afternoon. She should not play solitaire. She obeyed the warning and moved a little closer to a couple who seemed oblivious to the world. She did not feel hungry and felt no compelling push to visit the animals and laugh at their antics. The plants around her had a soothing effect, that aspect of nature always brought out her aesthetic appreciation. Maybe it was the greenery which spoke of new life and new beginnings and evoked a sense of the presence of the Great Being, or the different hues which sprung from the greenery and reminded one of the diverse personalities of people which all had one thing in common: dependence on the earth for substance. Even in her present state, the plants beckoned to her. She got up and went over to a large clump of ferns which were standing guard around a dignified pine which was too proud to remain at their level. She touched the one nearest to her, reminding herself that ferns were no flowering plants and as such had an affinity with her as she had lost her flower, before it was fully opened.

Deidre-Ann spotted a stone bench close to where she had been sitting and moved to it instead. She forced her folder into her bag and rested it on the bench beside her. She suddenly remembered the eight thousand dollars she had collected to pay for the books and hurriedly checked to see if it was still in her bag. It was all there and as she closed the bag, she got a strange feeling that she was being watched. Nervously she shot up and scanned the area around her but saw nothing suspicious, everyone was going about his or her business and seemed not to have noticed her. She sat down uneasily and a thought came to her. She looked around furtively and then took out the money and hid it in her bosom.

She had a smaller amount in her pocket but decided to leave that there so that if she needed anything, she could easily reach it instead of digging into her bosom.

She settled back and stared over the grounds of the park, wondering where her mother and sister were. Her heart ached at the thought of their certain agony. She knew they would be searching for her and started dialing her mother's number, but stopped half way through. They could easily track her if she called and she could not face them at that moment.

A voice nearby jolted her back to the present. "Miss mi can beg you a money fi buy a food? Mi nuh eat nuttin from morning, hungry a buss mi neck!"

Deidre-Ann spun around sharply. The plaintive voice belonged to a teenager of about sixteen years old. His brown-sugar face was streaked with what looked like dirt, and hunger stared boldly from his small confused eyes as he scratched his red unkempt hair noisily. He was wearing a faded brown tee shirt, a pair of shorts that was in the winter of its day and a pair of dirty sneakers, colour unknown. "Please Miss, a beg you, please help me out. Everybody jus' a run mi an' mi really need some food." He stretched out his hand hopefully, expectantly.

Deidre-Ann's first impulse was to chase him away. He was the last type of humanity that she wanted around her, his kind was unpredictable, clinging prey that pestered and plagued the rest of society using poverty as a facade for their sickening state. She reached into her pocket, came up with a hundred dollars and quickly, dismissively, handed it to him.

He hesitated before almost grabbing it from her. He held it in his hand as if it was the most precious gift he had ever received. He looked at it, then at her, then at it again and then at her. He appeared to be studying her features, inscribing it in his memory for future reference.

Deidre-Ann turned her back to him hoping he would take the hint and go his way.

"T'ank you Miss. God bless you Miss. Long time since anybody give me a dollar Miss. God bless you forever Miss, I will not forget it nor forget your face, bye Miss!"

She did not turn around, but nodded. She could hear him moving away, his feet disturbing the leaves on the ground. She dismissed him from her thoughts and decided to focus on her own predicament. She had done what was called running away and her family and the police would be searching for her shortly. Where will I sleep tonight? she questioned herself, and what will I do tomorrow, and the next day and the next? She looked down at her shoes and suddenly realized that she was wearing her school uniform and that that in itself would make her more conspicuous. She had to get some clothes, but where? She did not really want to start spending the little money. She had not thought of all this when she had impulsively taken off on her own. She remembered that there was a clothes store in the park but wondered if she could really afford to buy any and deplete her precious sum. Still, she knew she had to get out of the uniform, someone would certainly call the school if she was seen wandering around in her uniform.

She got up and started walking around, stopping every now and again to touch a plant and look at the details of some of the flowers. Finally she made her way towards the area where items of clothing and toys were being sold. She noticed that there were some ON SALE signs posted in front of the shops. She made her way in and looked around. The type of clothing that she usually wore were too expensive and moreover she did not want anything to draw attention to herself. Already, two shop attendants were paying more than the necessary attention to her. She finally bought two cheap floral summer wear dresses and a few personal items.

While she was putting the dresses away in her bag, something fell to the ground. As she bent to pick it up, her heart lurched with gladness. It was her mother's ATM card. She had used it to pay her school fee and had forgotten to give it back to her. She wondered how much money was left on it. There was a machine in the administrative area and she joined the short waiting line. The security guard who manned the area stared at her. She averted her eyes and stared steadfastly in front of her. Her check revealed that there was quite a substantial amount of money. She withdrew four thousand dollars and hid the card in an inner bag pocket, knowing that she would become a prime target if the wrong persons knew about the card.

She went back to the store and bought another dress and then headed for the bathroom. She quickly changed out of her uniform. Out of the uniform she looked even more mature; she pulled back the hair from her face and combed it in one ponytail. She looked younger as she had hoped. She did not want any member of the opposite sex to become attracted to her, thinking she was eighteen or older, providing fodder for the male sex was not her intention. Before leaving the bathroom, she tucked her folder, uniform and two dresses into the carry-all bag the lady in the shop had given her. She felt thankful that it was stylish and seemed durable.

She found a semi-secluded area and sat down. The palms, which formed a semi-circle around the stone bench, had a calming effect on her. This was aided by the solemn soothing song of the pines inspired by the casual lazy wind which was half asleep. She ignored the activities around her and tried to put some rationale to her actions. She had run away from school and from home. Why? She did not really want to be in school because what she had feared the most had actually been realized; someone had recognized her and soon her story would be all over the school and everyone would either pity or ridicule her. She simply could not live with that. In addition, if she went back home her family would force her to go back to school, if it wasn't the present one then it would be another one somewhere and inevitably, the gossip machine would be activated again. It made no sense; her life had crumbled like a building without a proper foundation in an earthquake of great magnitude. She had lost all vestige of integrity, her savour was gone and she was good for nothing; spoilt goods, fit to be discarded. The epitome of it all was that she now had a history of mental illness. Who would ever want to have any kind of meaningful relationship with her? As if to confirm her musings, a dart of pain pierced her in the head, causing her to suspend her present thoughts. She rested her head on the stone bench and closed her eyes but rest did not come. Images of groping hands, huge, dirty, coarse hands grabbed her. She suppressed the surging scream by covering her mouth. She spluttered and spat, breathing hard and opening her mouth for added support.

While she was struggling, she felt a hand on her shoulder. She pushed it off roughly and jumped up ready to do battle. The hands belonged to a middle aged woman with a graying hairline. Her serious face revealed decades of struggle and strain which had chiseled deep lines at the side of her mouth and given her face an experienced look. Deidre-Ann moved away from her and tried to sum her up some more.

"Young girl, you seem to be in trouble, ah come over to see if ah could help you somehow." Her voice had a sincere ring which went undetected by Deidre-Ann. "You seem to be sick." She looked at Deidre-Ann as one would look at a child who could not express herself properly.

"I don't need any help, thank you." Deidre-Ann looked at her skeptically.

"At leas' let mi pray for you." The woman had a pleading look and tone.

"Why do you think I need your prayer?" Deidre-Ann backed further away from the woman, watching her face as she did so.

"A young girl, all by herself and ready to cry, surely need some prayer, won't hurt you at all, at all." Her voice was persuading, persistent.

"You can stay where you are and pray if you want to," Deidre-Ann told her, wanting to get rid of her. The woman made her feel uncomfortable. Her conscience was berating her for not praying consistently. Moreover, she did not really want just about anyone to be praying with her. She certainly would not allow her to put her hands on her. She hated hands, especially strange hands touching her; you never knew when they would do more than just touch. The woman moved closer to her, but she did not touch her. She prayed from her heart, obviously praying was something she loved and spent much time doing. Deidre-Ann listened to the petitions and thanks offered up. At least there was one person who did not want to pry and dig into her affairs but had her well-being at heart. She seemed to be in need, but she did not beg her for anything except to put God into her heart.

Deidre-Ann sat down again, forcing her thoughts to direct themselves to her family. She was indeed remorseful for the pain she knew she must be causing them. She imagined her mother's tearful face and her sister trying to be strong, consoling her and commanding her tears to stay at bay. She could also imagine Nathan, proactive and business-like, asking questions and following leads and everyone else wondering why lightning should strike twice in the same place, burning the same persons.

She shoved their pain aside and thought of her own. They had never been violated in the way she had been, no one had ever dehumanized them and stolen their will to live! What use was school to anyone, when people treated you as if you were scum multiplied by the largest number? She wanted to evaporate into nothingness, not sit like Job amongst the ashes, cursing the day when she was born. Trying to become part of society after committing the 'crime' of being raped was as difficult as an alien from another planet being accepted on Earth. Somehow she had sprouted antennae which were a signal of the defiled and defunct. The mark of the scorned was branded on her person, even some family members looked at you with a strange blend of sympathy and derision, and the unstated questions from others screamed at you:

*Why did she have to let that happen to her? She must have invited it on herself somehow. I wonder if she is crying foul because something did not go right in the relationship? I wonder if she caught anything from him or them? That's damaged goods you are looking at. Don't look her straight in the eyes or else she'll see what you are thinking.*

As the thoughts swirled in her head like a tornado, Deidre-Ann raised her head to heaven involuntarily and spoke in silence with the Unseen Being which resided there. You're up there, the Bible says, that you're omnipresent and omniscient and I believe it is so, but why did you allow evil to get the better of me and rob me of my life? You are supposed to take care of the innocent and the fatherless, because I don't know where my father is, but you do. If you wanted to, those men would not have touched me. But they did and more than touched they did, while you stood idly by! Are you in agreement with those who are silently shouting unstated questions at me? And surely, you are not a God of evil, so why do evil men get away with atrocities like these? Why couldn't you let me live a normal life like other girls? I wanted to finish high school and go to sixth form and university too! I had dreams too! Is it so wrong to have dreams? Why God, why? Why me, why me, why me?

The bright colours of the retiring afternoon looked down in mockery at her silent cries, and a gang of sparrows cheerfully winging their way from work proudly displayed different formations in the sky; the radiance of the fading afternoon providing the perfect backdrop for their performance.

A wayward cloud, filled with gusto, covered the face of the tired sun and adjourned the birds' performance, leaving in its wake the beginning of the frowning dusk.

# CHAPTER EIGHT

# Night In The Park

The dusk heralded the waiting evening which came in and presided with an even darker scowl than was present before. The scowl deepened as it spread over the city. It obscured the buildings and invited them to fall asleep until the new day wrestled preeminence from it. The scowl blackened and sent people scurrying silently for their places of abode. The plants hung their heads in silence and resigned themselves to sleep. They were disturbed only by the stealthy, frivolous tickle of the evening wind which came and went at intervals and then it too, tired of its own game, went to rest. The stray dogs borrowed themselves against the walls and roots of trees, trying to find a place of safety and warmth for the long night ahead. Those that were hungry went scrounging around hoping that the humans had mercifully left even a morsel for them to prevent their bones from becoming more prominent and burst through their skin. They attacked the uncollected garbage with ferocity, ripping apart the boxes and food wrappers, their canines savagely exposed in the dark, the dire hunger masked by the shroud of darkness.

The street lights suddenly rocketed into being humming a song, which was often sung by bees and other unidentified insects. Its presence was eerie and uncanny, welcomed by some and unwelcomed by others. The light bore through the domineering blanket of dark revealing the activities of the night, but the buildings and shaded areas conspired to conceal some of the activities. Like a television suddenly flicked on with a show in progress, everyone was caught in action. The dogs with their feet on garbage containers continued their search for food and overturned the bins, making a hollow sound which reverberated through the evening. The sound of the vehicles snuffed out the swift stab and the heavy fall of shoes on the sidewalk.

Deidre-Ann hugged her bag closer to her chest, contemplating her next move. Indecisiveness frustrated her movements and plagued her mind. Now that the darkness had come, running away from home did not feel like such a good idea anymore. She missed the protective walls of her home and even though she resented the authority of those in her home, at that moment home seemed like a haven. She could not go back now, not when they would force her to go back to that hateful school and those that poured censure on the innocent. She had to find a way of surviving in obscurity, when it became too much then she would perhaps decide on the ultimate escape from life.

She thought of going to a hotel for the night, at least she had enough money but she knew that her age would probably pose a problem. She did not want to be questioned, investigated and handed over to her mother or a state institution as an uncontrollable teenager. Her best plan of action was to see what the streets had to offer and then plan accordingly. She felt nervous and prayed that she would not suffer an anxiety attack.

She stayed where she was, hunger and anxiety gnawing at the core of her being, hoping that no one would notice her or take an abnormal interest in her. She shifted into the shadow of a plant that reached over the fence and offered silent protection from the preying eyes of the street.

Loneliness pulled her out of hiding and she walked a little way from the fence. She was not alone. The street, earlier peopled only by intermittent sound of vehicles, was slowly coming to life. Earlier in the day she had noted that there was a gap in the fence which was being protected by a sheet of ply. As she ambled closer to that section, she noticed that the ply had been removed and that it had become a thoroughfare for some people who were walking in and out as if it were a gate.

From the street light she realized that these people who walked out always returned through the gap; there seemed to be some activity taking place inside. She sidled closer to the opening expecting to be stopped and questioned by those going in and out. She peeped through the hole and noticed that some people were lying on the ground while some were simply standing or walking around. She wondered why they were all there and after casting a furtive glance over her shoulders and waiting until the pedestrian traffic had ceased, she ventured through the gap in a timorous manner.

Once inside, she drew herself into a corner and tried to understand what was happening around her. The light was not as bright as it was from outside but she could still see. The people were obviously street people who made their bed in the park. They were of both sexes and ranged from the young to the elderly. A few had assumed the fetal position and seemed to be already asleep. Their mattresses were bits of cardboard or cloth. Some of them hugged bundles of plastic bags close to them, while some used them as pillows. Those asleep appeared to be the more elderly, the younger ones were sitting around in small groups or by themselves. She heard a sound to her left and when she looked around she saw a couple locked in an embrace. She moved away from them and in doing so, bumped into someone.

"Oh excuse me! Sorry!" she muttered apologetically, trying to step out of the way, but only managed to bump into the person again. "I really am sorry!" she exclaimed, moving away in the opposite direction.

"Ah rite, don't bodder yuself. Since you not trying to tief from mi." It was a suspicious female voice.

"Thief, no, no, I am not a thief!" Deidre-Ann hurriedly explained.

The girl stopped and walked back over to Deidre-Ann and looked at her from head to toe in an envious manner.

"Yuh new pan di street. Ah neva see yuh before. But a how yuh a speak so! English an' all and yuh clothes luk good, an' yuh hair comb up good, yuh a spy? Yuh come fi report wi to di park people dem?" Her dark eyes seemed too bright and piercing, they made Deidre-Ann uncomfortable. The prominent curved scar which ran from beneath her left eye to her neck caused Deidre-Ann to shiver in the warm night air.

"No! No, I am not a spy. I just happen to need a place for the night just like everybody else here!" she hastily explained, slowly retreating from the denouncing voice.

"But wat di likes of yuh doing out here? Yuh a look little business?" She edged back closer to Deidre-Ann, her piercing eyes cutting into her heart.

Deidre-Ann shivered again; maybe it would be better to go back out on the road. She looked towards the gap and started moving towards it, but the resentful voice halted her steps.

"If yuh a look a place fi di night, out on the street is not di place! It betta yuh stay inside here an' tek yuh chance!" She offered the advice grudgingly. She fixed her with a steely stare. "Unless yuh really a look little business!"

"I don't know what you mean!" Deidre-Ann protested.

"If yuh a pretend to be innocent ah really can't help yuh. If a nuh business yuh a look, it will do yuh good fi look out a yuh eye dem, listen wid yuh ears hole an' t'ink wid yuh head which nuh only mek fi hair grow pan it. If yuh have sense cause people dat look like yuh usually nuh have none! If yuh have sense an' look outa yuh eye hole dem, yuh might survive a little!"

She walked off after delivering her words of wisdom. Deidre-Ann stayed where she was for a while, considering the words and then she moved to a corner to continue her surveillance and summation. The place had a distinctive odour, the repugnant odour of dirty unwashed bodies, mixed with the smell of urine, stale food and heavens knew what else. Deidre-Ann moved as far away as she could from the 'Night Dwellers'. She thought of going back on the road but did not want to be outside by herself. At all costs, she had to prevent a re-occurrence of her tragedy, it must never happen to her again and she would fight the best way she knew how to prevent the 'Innocence Snatchers' from striking again.

She pulled a text book from her bag, sat on it and leaned against the wall. It was cold, craggy and uncomfortable. The ground around her was damp and sticks and stones dug into her flesh. She shifted from side to side but the effect was the same. She changed position and found it was the same, so she took out two more of her text books and rested her legs on them. She soon realized that she had a neighbour, when she heard a wracking, gut wrenching cough that must have shaken the person to the sole of his or her feet. Frightened at the sound, Deidre-Ann jumped up and hurriedly looked around her. It belonged to a young woman who was lying listlessly on the ground. Her possessions were hidden in a few scandal bags and she was lying on a torn old sheet.

"Oh sorry, I didn't see you," Deidre-Ann said, backing away and hurriedly bending to take up her belongings.

"Don't run away!" the woman begged. "I..." She launched off into another bout of coughing.

Deidre-Ann quickly moved her things a little distance away but something about the woman's forlorn form tugged at her heart. "You sound very sick," Deidre-Ann commented when the coughing had ceased and the young woman had stopped flailing her limbs.

"Yes ah really sick and everybody always run weh from me." The coughing threatened to erupt again but she covered her mouth with her hand and stifled it.

"Why, what is wrong with you?" Deidre-Ann questioned, sympathy building up inside her.

"If ah tell you, yuh ah go run away, an' sometime ah really need somebody fi talk to!" She suppressed another paroxysm of coughing.

Deidre-Ann knew the dangers of a person coughing on another so she stayed where she was, not too far but near enough to hear what the woman was saying. "I am not going to run away right now, I have nowhere to really run to." She surprised herself, saying this to a total stranger. "What is wrong with you?" she asked again.

"Ah have a t'ing dat everybody dread, dat everybody 'fraid of, even di docta! Ah have AIDS!" She made her last statement with such finality that Deidre-Ann was stumped for words. She did not know what to say. She had never met anyone with AIDS before. She took a closer look at her. She did not look different from any other human being she had ever met, only more sick, hopeless and lost. Her recent ordeal provided her with the means to empathize. She knew what it was like to feel less than a dog, but she was reticent about revealing this to a stranger. Instead of expressing her true feelings, she blinked back the tears that were threatening to break free and asked instead, "How did you get it?"

"My husband." There was a distant, cold chilling sound that accompanied the way she said the word. "I always stay home, an' do ebryting, ebryting an' ah didn't even know sey 'im out a road a carry on until 'im tek sick bad bad an' di doctor dem test him an' say 'im have it an' when ah do my test mi have it too." Her story was interrupted by a wave of coughing. Deidre-Ann's heart reached out to her but she turned her back, afraid of anything catching her. She hid her face against the wall, overcome with thankfulness that she had been spared from that eventual death sentence.

The bout of coughing over, the woman laid still, sapped of the strength to talk. Deidre-Ann wanted to say something to comfort her, but she had been silenced by the realness of the situation.

It was the woman who broke the stifling silence. "You sleeping or you fraid, which one?" The voice was low and feeble.

"No I'm not sleeping, I was just thinking." It was the truth. She was thinking about human pain and suffering and wondering why the innocent always seemed to suffer most. "So what happen to your husband in the end and why are you now on the street instead of at a place where you can get help?"

"Well Miss, 'im dead soon afta the doctor fine 'im out an' since 'im was the one paying the rent an' I never had a job, ah had was to leave the house. Since ah had AIDS nobody nuh want me live with them, so..." Her voice petered off, the physical pain and the embarrassment rendering her silent.

Deidre-Ann thought she was sleeping and did not trouble her with any more questions. She herself was becoming sleepy, so she closed her eyes hoping to get some sleep.

A weak voice drifted across to her. "So wat yuh doing on the street?"

Deidre-Ann startled, jerked out of the sleep that had been creeping over her. "What did you say?" she asked, yawning and turning towards the woman.

"Wat yuh doing on the street? Yuh look pretty an' sound educated, dis is not the plais for yuh!"

"I'm having some problems at home and I need to sort out myself," Deidre-Ann replied evasively, not wanting to tell anyone her real story.

"The street not the place for dat. Yuh have to move around watching every move even when yuh a sleep yuh have to watch, one eye always have to open."

The warning was not lost on Deidre-Ann and was not given too early either. There were the sounds of vehicles stopping close to the gap and the people in the park became very quiet as if they were waiting for something.

"What is happening?" Deidre-Ann whispered loudly to the woman. "Everyone is sitting up and some people are gathering their things."

She looked towards the woman and realized that she was slowly trying to raise herself. "Sometimes the park people dem come an' run us out an' sometimes other people come."

"Other people? Who are other people and what do they want with street people?" The whole thing did not make sense to Deidre-Ann.

"Girl yuh too simple!" There was honest bewilderment in the woman's voice. "They come for bwoy and gal alike an' carry dem weh. Sometimes dem come back, sometimes dem nuh come back! Yuh understand now!" The surprise was still in her voice.

"Yes, yes, I understand," Deidre-Ann replied, new and dangerous knowledge rushing out at her. She got up and held her bags close to her, on the alert like everyone else.

Two men came through the gap. They were obviously not street people based on their appearance. A third man, one from among the street people, came forward, had a whispered conversation and then left with the men.

As soon as they were gone, things went back to normal, but Deidre-Ann became afraid. The urge to sleep had withdrawn itself and she found herself doing what the first girl had warned her to do; look out of her eyes, listen with her ears and think with her head.

She got up and stood with her bags in her hands. Her neighbour had gone to sleep, her body not able to withstand the rigors of sleeplessness. Deidre-Ann soon realized that two young men had edged close to her and seemed to be watching her. An alarm clanged ceaselessly in her brain as her discomfort heightened. The men did not move.

Soon there was the sound of another vehicle stopping close to the gap. This time only one man came through the gap. The two men went to meet him and Deidre-Ann started edging away from the wall, trying not to step on any of the sleeping forms. She was 'watching out of her eyes' and saw when the three men stopped where she had stood before. They looked around and one shouted out, "Anybody see di new girl? She did jus' deh yah suh!"

No one answered him so they started searching for Deidre-Ann who was trying to hide behind three people who had got up to watch what was going on. One of them was the girl whom she had stumbled into earlier on.

"Wat you looking for di new girl fah? She did tell yuh seh she a look nobody? Tell me she did aks yuh fi look nobody fi har!" Her voice was loud and intimidating. She was obviously not afraid of the men.

"If she no want nobody wat she a do pan di street den?" a gruff voice demanded.

"Dat is fi har business not yours; a bet yuh one a yuh can't touch her tonight unless she want yuh to. Man jus' cut from ya so or else... yuh never hear bout mi yet?"

The visitor seemed frightened and turned to go, but the young men blocked his way and held out their hands menacingly. He dipped his hands into his pocket, gave them some money and ran through the gap.

# CHAPTER NINE

# After Deidre-Ann Runs Away

"This place really needs cutting and the hedge is so overgrown!" Mrs. Lenworth exclaimed as she got out of the car with Ashley.

"Ever since Ann's problem started and we're not around much, the gardener don't come around to do his job," Ashley said, surveying the weed-choked flower gardens. Some of the smaller plants were completely smothered by weeds and were bravely fighting to escape their grasp by crawling on the ground, but the weeds had cornered them, blocking off their escape.

"But Ashley, you don't remember that the regular gardener went back to St. Elizabeth. His arthritis had got worse and another one recommended by the Gayles' next door had taken his place." Mrs. Lenworth frowned, trying to remember the details. Her mind was no longer focused on the mundane. Deidre-Ann's disappearance had relegated things such as gardening unimportant.

"Yes Mummy, that's true, but we did not get to meet him, he came once when we were not here and I asked Mrs. Gayle to pay him. The one that has been coming now and again is really Marla's people gardener, but he claims he already has enough to do so he barely has time to squeeze us in," Ashley reported.

"Mr. Gayle usually knows how to find domestic help, I am going to call him and ask him to find somebody for us," Mrs. Lenworth said, opening the verandah grill.

"I don't think Mr. Gayle is there. I was talking to Mrs. Gayle the other day and she said he is doing business abroad and when he is not abroad, he does business elsewhere, so he is hardly around," Ashley pointed out as she walked into the living room.

"Now that you say it, I couldn't tell when last I've seen him. Since Ann's problem I hardly have time to socialize with my neighbours." Mrs. Lenworth hissed her teeth and sighed heavily.

"I think Nathan might know somebody or even let us use his gardener," Ashley suggested, falling wearily into the first chair in the living room.

It had been a most tiring afternoon, driving all around town trying to find Deidre-Ann. Now the dusk had handed over to night and it was impossible to find her now. This nightmare was far from over, she thought. With Deidre-Ann regaining her mental faculties and going back to school, she had thought that the worst had been pushed behind them. She was naïve in thinking that her sister had got over her ordeal, and that everything would be a pleasant walk along the garden path, but at the same time she had not envisioned Deidre-Ann running off. She chided herself for not noting the cracks and taking her seriously when she objected to going to school. As far as she had figured, hiding away from society was not the way to get Deidre-Ann to shake her fear of people and their taunts and silent accusations. She was obviously wrong, the whole family had been wrong. Where was Deidre-Ann, she agonized, and what had made her run off? Her old school was nowhere near the new one and Nathan had kept the incident out of the news not wanting to further sully her character. She wondered if anyone had recognized her, pointed her out and said anything to her. That fear had been hounding her all along but she had relegated it to the remotest part of her head, ignoring it every time it sought to break free. Now it was forced out by Ann's disappearance.

She heard a sound and turned around to the sofa which was close to her. Her mother was lying on it with her face turned in. She had been so absorbed in her reverie, that she had no idea her mother had not gone to her room. She always hated being alone whenever there were problems. Ashley moved over to her, the sobs causing her body to shudder. As Ashley hugged her, the sobs became louder and almost wrenched her heart from its place. Ashley thought that her mother should not be going through this again. Once was enough, all those months of sleeplessness and going to the hospital for hours, the mental and physical anguish, the fight to keep her personal life separate from her career; it was just too much. She muttered comforting words to her, but soon she herself was sobbing along with her.

Would they ever see Ann again? Where was she at this moment? Was she walking the streets of the city, confused and lost? What if she got sick again? Did the strange man posing as her father have anything to do with her disappearance? Were the students at her new school privy to her situation? Who was the person who kept calling the house, even after the number had been changed? The last question seemed to trigger off the telephone, because it started to ring persistently, urgently as she thought about it. Ashley ignored it at first, not knowing whether it was news about her sister or the threats coming in. It stopped after a while and then started again. Mrs. Lenworth, as if awakening out of her sobbing, tried to pull herself out of her daughter's embrace to answer it, but Ashley gently pushed her back into the sofa and went to answer it herself. Whoever it was, she did not want her mother to have to deal with him.

She took it in the kitchen instead of the living room and held it away from her as if trying to keep the caller away from her.

"Hello." She little more than whispered into the telephone. Her voice sounded uninterested and condescending.

"You getting fresh and bright, why you tek so long to answer di phone?" A muffled heavy breathing defiled her hearing, willing her to reply. Instead, she kept quiet. "So you playing with me? When I finish with all of you, you will see who playing or who serious. The gal a sleep nuh, tell her to sleep on cause ah know where she going now. Is only a matter of time before ah ketch up with her an' you too!' The scurrilous voice, obviously disguised, seemed to be reaching for her, trying to unbalance her.

"Why don't you leave us alone, you cowardly dog? What did we ever do to you?" Ashley screamed in a whisper over the telephone.

"Oh so you a try curse me off! Guess what, more than ever now, yuh corner dark!" The abrasive tone was rising in anger, threatening to shout at her.

Ashley, no longer trying to appease him as she had done on previous calls, cursed him in a loud whisper, "Go away dog, you are not a man, only dogs rape women!" Incensed, she put down the telephone and stood glaring at it, as if it was the offensive caller. She stood looking at it for a while and the unanswered questions crowded her mind. Who was this person and how did he manage to get their number? She asked herself these questions every time he called but had no way of answering them, only a mocking echo kept taunting her mind.

She went back into the living room and saw her mother sitting up, the sobs had quietened but silent tears meandered down her face, uncertain of their course.

"Who was that?" she asked, her voice hoarse and barely audible.

"Just someone from campus," she lied, evading her mother's gaze. "Wanted to find out about an assignment." She compounded the lie, wanting to be more convincing so as to stem the questioning.

"Okay," Mrs. Lenworth responded, "thought it might be someone with something important to tell us." She looked forlornly at her daughter and then went towards the bathroom.

"Mummy, can I get you anything? We didn't really have any dinner, remember?" Her voice had a coaxing note.

"Food! Eat! Good God no! Not even a crumb could pass my throat now, I would be sure to choke on it." She shook her head dismissively and continued walking to the bathroom.

Ashley spoke to her receding back. "Just the same here. I only want a drink." She could not imagine enjoying food when Ann was out there somewhere, hungry and depressed, away from her family.

Later, she got into bed with her mother. In times of such pain they did not need separate beds. Sleep kept itself from them. They tossed and turned, each with her own thoughts yet bonded by the same indescribable pain which was eating at their hearts.

"Mummy," Ashley spoke softly, hesitantly to her mother. "Mummy do you think we should pray? Do you think that God would listen to us, he has certainly kept his distance from us for quite a while now." The criticism and futility were evident in her voice.

"We never know if He will consider us seeing that we are in such distress. He is supposed to care for us," Ashley continued, trying to convince her mother as well as herself.

"Well I can see no harm in it." She sounded dubious. "Strange things have happened in this life. Maybe this strange situation will cause Him to help us."

"Help us again," Ashley interjected without thinking. "Things were really not so bad before Ann's trouble."

"You seem to be forgetting the trouble with your father!" The bitterness had seeped into her voice and was threatening to spill itself.

Ashley detected it and tried to steer her away from it. "Mummy please let us try and forget him now, Ann is in more trouble and since we cannot find her, then we have to ask someone bigger than us to help us."

Without saying another word, they got down from off of the bed and prayed, each silently. Ashley prayed for her father as well. It was a good thing her mother did not know because she would probably have stopped praying.

Ashley could not sleep even after her mother fell into a fitful sleep, tossing and calling Deidre-Ann. She started to relive the incidents starting from the family forcing Deidre-Ann to go back to school and her disappearance that afternoon. It had started during the summer holidays after her mother had gone ahead and registered her for the new school.

"Ann I registered you for school today. I hope you will love your new school." She looked at her nervously and waited for the expected explosion.

"School? What school? Who told you I want to go back to any old school?" Deidre-Ann was furious. She looked at her mother as if she had betrayed her.

"But Ann you can't just stay home for the rest of your life. I know it is difficult but you will just have to try and get back your life." Mrs. Lenworth was begging, pleading with her.

"Mummy I know you are embarrassed about having a daughter who will not make you proud because she will not finish school and go to university, but you are not the one who has a poster sticking to your back and front that says, 'Look out everyone, here comes the girl that was raped, stay away from her. She's dirty!'" She turned her back to everyone and continued to watch the television.

Ashley came to her mother's aid. "Ann I know what you are feeling but remember the whole family is with you, and was with you throughout everything, we only want the best for you. We ..."

"Yes, you want me to have the best of the scorn and dirty names. You seem not to remember that in this land of wood and water, the raped is the criminal and the rapist the victim!" She glared at her sister, daring her to dispute what she regarded as a fact.

"Ann I am not going to stand here and pretend that I don't know what you are talking about. We are all aware that the police and others in the legal field ask questions that really make victims feel embarrassed, but..."

Deidre-Ann pounced on her, not allowing her to finish. "Since you know so much, what is your problem? It is only because I was supposed to be dead why they did not accuse me of begging to be raped. I heard about the bad treatment given to women from this society and I don't expect to be treated any differently!" She pouted and turned her back, unwilling to listen to any entreaty.

"Ann when all is said you can't just throw away your life! What has happened to the fighter we once had? The one who did not allow the whole world to bother her or tell her what she can and cannot achieve! Where did the salt go?"

"It went with my demise! I am alive yet dead, breathing yet being stifled. I am a shell, my inside is gone. School is not going to make me a person again!" Her voice was pathetic, the old Deidre-Ann was gone, her saltiness washed away in the rain on the eventful night.

"Well Ann," Mrs. Lenworth came back into the argument, "as your mother I just can't sit here and allow you to really die or become a part of the fixtures of this house, you have to use your brains and realize your dreams. You can't just sit around and become what you want to be!" She walked over to her and tried to hug her but she pushed her away.

The begging and pleading continued and other family members got involved over the summer period. They managed to convince Deidre-Ann to go back to school, but now Ashley was not certain it was the best thing they had done. It would have been better to have her just sitting around than not to have her at all. She was certain that she had ran off because something or someone had hurt her. Where on earth was she? If she was not careful, the same thing could happen to her again. Ashley put up a mental block on that thought; it would be just too much.

She knew her mother would probably hit her, if she knew what she had been trying to do for some months now. She had been trying to contact her father. For some reason she believed that he should know what was going on in their lives. She felt that somehow he would make a difference. She had visited his workplace but they said he no longer worked there. His secretary of many years told her that he said he was going into another field as he was tired of the real estate business. He did not disclose what it was, but had intimated that it would sometimes take him out of the island. She had not seen him in three years and neither had his long time school friend, Mr. Greaves.

She had never mentioned it to her mother as she feared the back lash, but she did miss her father. She remembered the frequent outings and the little gifts and stories. She also remembered the nights when he came home late, too late for Ann and herself to spend time with him. She also remembered the furious arguments between her mother and himself in the mornings after his late nights. Never to be forgotten was the night he went away. She had waited up all evening because she wanted to ask him to help her with her special science project that night, but he did not come home until after eleven o'clock. When he came, before she could approach him, the war started. Derogatory words and select expletives were hurled at each other without any consideration for the children or neighbours who had congregated by their gates or were peeping over their fences to get better access to the late night tirade, a clear source of entertainment for them.

Ashley felt that if her father was at home, things would not have gone so terribly awry. One of the most important questions on her mind was, where was he and who was the man impersonating him? Why had he gone to Ann's school? How did he know she was there and did he have anything to do with her disappearance? The questions and flashbacks kept assaulting her. She tried to push them away and summon sleep but they were persistent and kept badgering her. Finally, sleep conquered the thoughts and they succumbed for a while and then attacked again in the form of nightmares where bearded men were chasing Deidre-Ann.

# CHAPTER TEN

# Deidre-Ann On The Road

The lights of the city were every where, beaming down bravely from tall light posts and illuminating the area. There were neon lights which colourfully flashed the names of goods and services from their stationery posts. There had been a moderate shower earlier and the lights were dancing on small pools of water, striking them at an angle, and then bouncing off into the atmosphere. The tyres screeched and screamed as they hit the water and made a dull 'splashing' sound which sent the water shooting off in all directions and placing the pedestrians in danger.

The buildings stood silently, observing the activities of the streets. Vehicles rushed headlong purposefully in all directions, unmindful of the activities around. There were a number of people, mostly young ones, walking along, some holding hands and conversing, some walking alone going faster than the couples. A few seemingly homeless people merged with those moving along. Their steps were slow, halting and purposeless. After all, they were really not going anywhere; time had no meaning to them. Morning, afternoon, evening and night were time divisions for the purposeful, but for the vagrants they lacked importance. Even worse than the vagrants were the mindless ones who perceived nothing but moved along even slower, their bodies tuned only to the inbuilt natural reactions of a human.

Deidre-Ann stood at a bus stop observing it all. At the moment, she was like the vagrants, not going anywhere in particular. She was in a state of limbo, simply standing and watching the activities around her. After spending the day walking around and pretending to shop and trying to keep clear of the crowds, Deidre-Ann was tired. She definitely was not going back to the park and wanted to try her luck with a hotel for the night. Commuters using the bus stop came and went, but Deidre-Ann stayed where she was as if she was a part of the fixtures of the bus stop. At times she went unnoticed, but at other times people stared at her or tried to start a conversation. One young man stayed a very long time at the bus stop and Deidre-Ann wondered if he too were homeless, but changed her mind when she saw how he was dressed. Very soon, she realized that he was edging closer to her. Panic was born immediately, but soon waned when she realized that they were not alone.

"My name is Tirel Anderson, what is yours?"

Her only response was to move away from him.

"Ah notice you standing up here a long time now, what happen, somebody stood you up or you don't have anywhere to go?"

She could not be certain whether he was serious or mocking her. She only knew that the bitterness she had developed for the opposite gender was heightening, and if he came any nearer to her, she was going to hit him. "Look boy, get lost," she said in a low, threatening voice.

"Oh so you can talk, yuh not a dummy!" he exclaimed, mocked shock in his voice.

Again she did not respond but pulled farther away from him.

"So you're not telling me your name?" he persisted, not daunted by her unfriendliness.

He drew closer to her and impulsively, she took off her left shoe. Apparently, the young man did not see the action and took the insult for an invitation. Deidre-Ann hit him once, then twice before he realized what was happening. He uttered an expletive, made a low grunt of pain and covered his face for a moment.

Deidre-Ann was off before he could react. She walked quickly down the street, rushing past some people who were walking on the sidewalk. The young man was coming quickly after her, cursing as he came along, but she did not turn around. She came to a stoplight and thought it would be best to go to the other side of the street. The light was on green but it would soon turn to amber. Normally she would not have chanced crossing, but she did not stop to think, knowing that the enraged young man was close behind her. She flashed across the road without looking back, and when she was a little more than half way across, the light changed and she hastily ran across. When her feet hit the sidewalk she looked back and saw the young man standing on the other side. He had started crossing but had to run back when the vehicles suddenly started moving. Counting her blessings, she walked swiftly down the street, clutching her bags. She cast furtive glances behind her, but could not tell whether the young man was following because that area had quite a number of people who all appeared to be moving swiftly in the same direction.

She half-ran and half-walked and turned on the adjacent street, looking back all the time. No one seemed to be following, so she slowed down and bent over, almost out of breath. If it had been during her cheerleading years, the exercise would not have been so tiring. As soon as her breathing became normal, she moved on because a few people had slowed down to ask if she was alright. She answered in the affirmative and moved off again. She didn't like that street because some of the lights were out and there were areas of semi-darkness. She walked at the edge of the street instead of the side-walk. Who knew who, or what, would jump out at her. She was not street-wise, but her senses were all alert. Her past experiences had taught her to be wary and had awakened the fighting instinct within her, which was ironic, since some of the time she was not too interested in living as it took too much effort.

Without incident, she came to a four way street. She stopped shortly, trying to make up her mind which one to take. She had no idea where in the city she was, what she would do and where she would go. She considered staying in a hotel for the night, but unless she took a taxi, she could not get to the few that she knew about. She wondered which would be the greater evil: walking around until she found a place or taking a taxi. There were too many stories about taxi drivers taking away young girls. She would try to find one that would take her to one of the hotels, but she would not charter it. It would have to be one of the regulars running on the route, that way there would be other people in it. She wondered where she would find such a taxi since she had no idea where she was, and where these taxis were parked. Moreover, it was almost 10:00 p.m. and not many people were around.

She made a left turn and walked up the street. The street was brightly lit and there were a few people moving around. She looked around for the friendly face of an adult who could guide her. She walked slowly, trying to peer into people's faces without seeming to do so. She did not want a confrontation or people getting the wrong impression about her.

She saw a couple holding hands and moved towards them. Before she was right beside them, a group of boys came rushing up the street. They seemed to be dragging something or someone between them. Deidre-Ann moved behind the couple and looked at the scene before her.

"Pass up di money bwoy or else you will get a board coffin!" one of the boys shouted at the boy they had been dragging between them. His coarse voice caused Deidre-Ann to cringe in fear. She would certainly hate to tangle with him. He was wearing a short pants and a tee shirt. His features were not clearly defined, but Deidre-Ann noted that he was tall, sturdy and imposing. He wrenched the smaller boy from the others and dragged him towards him. The boy was standing on tip-toe with his head almost pressed against the older boy's chest.

"Ah don't have no money. Ah use one bill to buy food an' when ah did put down the res' beside the spare bottle a wata and go clean a car winda, when mi come back mi neva see it," the accused boy mumbled, sobbing all the time.

"But how come yuh neva tell nobody 'bout that or ask if anybody did tek the money!" another boy said.

"Yes mi did ask but everybody seh is not them," the boy said weakly, trying to free himself from his captor.

"Is what yuh doing, trying to get weh from me?" the older boy asked, holding him even tighter. "Ah notice that from the other day some a you little bwoy a get t'ief an' a use off di money weh all a you suppose to give me." He paused and hit the boy across his face. "As from tonite, dat done! A mi rule dis part a the street and when mi give order, nobody mus' dis!" The boy screamed as his brain received the pain. Deidre-Ann felt as if she had been hit too. She wanted to rescue the boy but knew they would only turn on her. No one seemed concerned as the few people around passed by without halting, minding their own business. The couple who Deidre-Ann was hiding behind continued to hold hands and speak in low tones, seemingly unperturbed, or perhaps they were accustomed to street brawls.

"Okay give him a chance," one of the boys said. "Him sort a new to dis t'ing, an' sometimes some of the bwoy dem really t'ief from the little one dem."

"You better mind yourself!" The captain turned around and glared at him. "Mine you get a beaten tonite!"

The boy did not answer but backed away from the group a little. The prospect of a beating did not seem attractive to him. The big boy turned back his attention to the boy that he was holding.

"This is the last warning fi yuh. If you violate or disrespect again yuh not gwine live long!" He hit him again and the slap sounded loud and hollow in the absence of motor vehicles.

The boy screamed and the older boy released him suddenly. He fell backwards, hitting the side of his head. For a while, he laid still. The gang looked on and then walked away without a backward glance. Only one boy remained, the one who had spoken out in defense of the boy. He sat beside him and raised him up, putting his arms around him. The boy kept falling to one side like an empty sack. Deidre-Ann almost went to help him but thought better of it. So this was life on the street! Home started to seem like a safe place, but she could not go back now until they were prepared to see things her way, but would they ever?

The couple had moved away while Deidre-Ann was watching the brawl. She looked around for anyone else who appeared to be trustworthy but did not see anyone she wanted to talk to. A few persons were still standing around and Deidre-Ann figured they must be waiting on some form of transportation. She decided to wait and see what they were up to.

Soon a taxi pulled up and the driver pushed his head through the window and shouted out "Fenton Boulevard! Fenton Boulevard! Last trip for the night!" Six people rushed forward and tried to squeeze into the taxi, but he could only take five. The odd one came back to the pavement looking annoyed and disappointed. Deidre-Ann looked around and realized that there were only six of them still standing on the pavement. She decided that when the next taxi came, she would not be the one left standing in that strange lonely place.

Five minutes later, the next taxi arrived. All six persons seemed to have had the same idea about not being left behind. The driver had no need to shout out his destination as no sooner had he screeched to a halt, everyone pushed forward. Deidre-Ann found herself pushing against another girl to get into the back. The bag on her back and the one in her hand hampered her somewhat but despite being savagely pushed, she got inside. As the taxi pulled away, she looked in disbelief as she saw the same young man who had failed to get a place in the previous taxi, standing alone and forlorn.

She cast sidelong glances at the people in the taxi, wondering if they were going close to the Fenton Hotel. She had gone there once with her mother and she had enjoyed the ambience. The compound was neatly kept with the flower gardens all kept in check and the paths all neatly paved and swept and bordered by flowering shrubs, all meticulously shorn. The prospect of a good bath and a warm bed was more than enticing to her. Her real problem was whether the driver was going that far or not. She didn't really want to ask him and draw attention to herself. There was silence in the taxi, no one seemed to have anything to discuss, or maybe it was due to the state of the society where everyone mistrusted the next person especially if he or she was a stranger. Even the notorious taxi drivers were sometimes suspicious of the passengers and were refusing to take them to particular destinations. Deidre-Ann watched anxiously as the passengers got off one by one. Soon there was only one passenger besides herself left. She decided that whether or not she got to the hotel she was not going to be the only passenger left with the driver. She timidly asked, "Driver how far away is the Fenton Hotel?"

"Only about ten minutes drive away," he responded quickly. "Are you going there?"

"Yes, I want to go there. How much does it cost?"

He told her and the silence settled in again.

"Driver beg you stop after you cross over the next stoplight," the other passenger said and looked away outside the window as the stoplight loomed in sight.

After he had gone through the stoplight, the driver stopped and the passenger got out. Realizing that she would be alone with the driver, panic spread across Deidre-Ann's body and she began to sweat profusely. She jumped out of the taxi before the driver started off and handed him the fare through the window.

"But Miss ah think you said you want to go to the hotel. It is just five minutes away!" He looked at her in astonishment, his inability to comprehend her behaviour written plainly on his face.

"Well, I changed my mind," Deidre-Ann said emphatically, moving away from him.

Instead of driving off, he stared at her as one would at an object which perplexed the mind and then he shouted at her receding figure. "I understand now why you have to get off here. Dis is where most of them stay." He laughed uproariously, hitting the steering wheel as he did so. "But you not dress right for the job!" He then sped away and his laughter was lost in the vulgar sound of the engine.

For a while Deidre-Ann stood as still as a lamppost, looking at the disappearing vehicle and wondering what the man's words and amusement were all about. She had no intention of going anywhere alone with any member of the opposite sex, if she could help it. It didn't matter what they said or did.

She turned her attention to her surroundings, a number of large buildings reared up on either side of her. They appeared to be in a competition to reach the sky first. They were protected by giant iron gates whose strength was manifested by the thickness of the steel used to construct the gates. The area was brightly lit by huge bulbs around which swarmed silly insects fighting to perch on the lamp. No sooner had they embraced the lamp, than they fell in a drunken stupor to the ground, but they just kept on going as if pulled by an unseen magnet. They reminded Deidre-Ann of repeat offenders who knew the penalty of breaking the law, but continued to do so nevertheless.

Raucous laughter pulled her attention away from the folly of the insects. She was hoping to see other people standing around waiting for taxis to come. She moved onto the sidewalk and came face to face with a number of girls. They seemed to be sharing and enjoying a joke among themselves. They were dressed outrageously, some of them almost wearing nothing but extremely short mini-skirts and shorts, some of them made of tight fitting mesh material, barely holding their bodies in place. Some appeared to be wearing only brassieres or tiny mid-riff sleeveless blouses. One girl sported a dress which was held together by gold loops: it covered only her breasts and other private areas. They all seemed to be wearing knee-high boots. Colourful wigs of all lengths completed the ensembles. Deidre-Ann was taken aback, she had an idea who they were and like a spark in the wilderness, knowledge of what the driver's words meant flashed across her mind. Shame and embarrassment flooded her face at the very thought that anyone could really think that she was that kind of person. She had to get away from the section quickly, to be in the same area as these girls only made her situation more acute. She walked hurriedly past and as she did so, the raucous laughter came to an abrupt end. Even though it was night, she could feel the eyes raking her from head to toe. She continued to walk swiftly and was breathing a sigh of relief when she came upon another small group. She hurried past again, but as she walked down the sidewalk, she observed that they seemed to have taken over the whole length of it. She didn't want to be in an area by herself, but she also didn't want to be anywhere near them. For heaven's sake, this was like something out of a story book!

She moved past another group of girls and found what she thought was an unoccupied spot. She stood there and looked anxiously down the road, hoping that a taxi with people would come by so that she could get away.

"Hi mum who yuh, an' why yuh park yuh body here so?" a voice assaulted her. It was filled with anger and threat.

"I am not staying here. I'm just waiting on a taxi," Deidre-Ann tried to explain quickly, hoping her aggressor would leave her alone.

"But who yuh really? The only taxi that park roun' yah suh is the man dem dat come to us." With each spoken word, her volume increased and Deidre-Ann feared that soon all the girls would swarm her like locusts.

"As I said, I'm only waiting for a taxi. I am not in this line of business." Deidre-Ann said the last sentence emphatically, hoping to be convincing.

"My girl if yuh not in dis business weh yuh a do on the street at dis time a the night by yourself?" The voice was now shrill.

Deidre-Ann felt fear and the beginning of a headache. Maybe if she just walked away she would not threaten the monopoly on the girl's space.

"Alright let me move from here," she said, turning to walk away, but the girl had become riled for more reasons than one and would not let her walk away so easily.

"Is here so yuh boss tell yuh to come. When him know that dis is our turf? Him mus' really be green in dis business and look how him tell her to dress!"

By now a number of girls had come to hear what the quarrel was all about. Since nothing was going on, the entertainment was welcome.

"But look how she dress and hear how she a talk like she better than us." This came from one of the girls who had joined in the fun.

"I'm not here to do business," Deidre-Ann repeated, trying not to let the nervousness in her voice escape. "I just want to get a taxi!" She held on tightly to the bag in her hand, looking for an opening to run but seeing none. She felt like an animal cornered by its predators.

"So since when taxi park over here?" an incredulous voice asked. "Is come yuh come to cut in on we business with yuh pretty talk an' yuh pretty face." She shoved Deidre-Ann, cementing the meanness in her voice.

"I just want to get a taxi. Let me out of here," she pleaded.

"Yes sure," said the girl who had started the whole scenario.

"I am going to let you out of here." She mimicked Deidre-Ann's accent, moving closer to her. "Ah going give you a message to tek back to you boss!"

Deidre-Ann saw a silver glint in her hand and before knowledge of what it was could hit her, the hand was raised to her face. She stepped back and shielded her face with her hand and gave a scream when she felt an intense burning pain.

"Jesus gawd Belris, you really cut her!" one of the girls bawled out, backing away.

"My gal, yuh a one wicked gal!" a male voice chimed in. "Yuh neva have to cut her, Jesus!"

"Me gone from here!" another voice rang out, frightened.

As if they were in agreement with her, the crowd dwindled away as quickly as it had gathered. Deidre-Ann was left bent over, the blood dripping from her hand like a tap that was not properly turned off.

"Let me help you, Miss," a gruff voice offered. Deidre-Ann looked up into the eager face of a tired, hungry-looking young man. There was a hint of meanness and toughness in his eyes but concern for her lessened these qualities.

Deidre-Ann shifted away from him because he was a male and she would never trust a man again in her life. "Just leave me alone!" she said, edging away even further, but she was beginning to feel faint.

"You need help, ah can help you." The boy was persistent. He moved over to her side, took out a dirty rag from his pocket and handed it to Deidre-Ann.

Deidre-Ann looked at the rag with scorn. "I ..." Her voice was cut short by the wail of a siren coming directly at them. The girls who had withdrawn to their former positions all started to scream and run in different directions. Deidre-Ann stood her ground, but when she remembered that even though she was not involved in prostitution, she was in the same area with the prostitutes and moreover she was a run-away. She was nonplussed at the turn of events and did not know which way to go. If she was caught by the police, she might be charged for prostitution and if she wasn't, she would have to go back home or else the police would want to send her to a reform school.

"Come with me!" It was an order, not a request. The boy was holding on to her hand like a vice grip and was pulling her after him.

Not having a chance, Deidre-Ann followed and not a moment too early. The police hit the sidewalk as the car jerked to a stop. But the girls, seeming to know the routine, had disappeared like a vapour in the air. The police searched briefly but did not find them. Deidre-Ann was placed behind a barrel close to the back of a building. The boy had clamped his dirty hand over her mouth to still the heavy breathing, but Deidre-Ann decidedly pushed it away and covered her mouth herself. She could hear the fall of the heavy boots as they searched in silence. She could almost reach out and touch one, so close did he come by her.

She had no idea how long she crouched in hiding, but soon she heard a gruff whisper, "Follow me" and her hand was arrested again as she was pulled along. There was something slightly familiar about the boy and Deidre-Ann searched her mind urgently trying to fit the face to a time and place. The pain prevented her from focusing on the boy's identity. It was excruciating, unrelenting, tearing through her hand as if it wanted to escape only to return each time. It was still bleeding, she could feel it oozing on to her dress and the section of her bag on that side. She didn't even know how bad the cut was, neither could she understand why she didn't just stop running and let the boy go on his way. She didn't want to be going anywhere with any of these lecherous non-human beings, but she didn't know where to go or what to do at the moment, so despite herself she followed blindly.

They had left the huge buildings and the well lit areas and were on a street with only a few street lights and much smaller buildings. It seemed to be a business area as most of the buildings had signs advertising clothes, betting games and grocery, among other things. Most of them were closed and the boy avoided the few that were open by keeping in the darkened areas or walking between the buildings, keeping close to the sides. At intervals, he would stop to enquire about Deidre-Ann's state and tell her to rest and then move on.

"Where are we going?" Deidre-Ann enquired, breathing hard. She uttered occasional moans, not wanting to seem like a cry baby by crying out.

"Ah taking yuh where somebody can help you," he answered without stopping.

"Why are you being kind to me? I don't like men," Deidre-Ann stated in a matter of fact way.

"Well you mus' hav' a good reason for saying dat, but is not all man bad. An' ah helping you because yesterday when ah was hungry, you help me out." His voice had a note of gratitude in it.

"Help you out yesterday?" Deidre-Ann responded and then it came back to her. "Oh that's why I was wondering where I had seen your face before. You were the boy at the gardens. What is your name?"

"Everybody call me Slinky. An' even though ah can't read dat well ah always remember ah face, especially if is a kind one." His tone had a pleased note at his assessment of himself. "Ah taking you to somebody who can fix up yuh hand an' tomorrow if it still bad, yuh can go to the doctor," he continued.

"But where do you live?" Deidre-Ann asked. They were going up a slight incline, pass some small mostly wooden structures huddling closely together in the slight night wind. He avoided the people who were sitting or standing outside, some dancing to the reggae music coming from one of the larger structures.

Finally they stopped. Slinky knocked on one of the doors and a middle-aged woman wearing a coloured head tie opened the door. Her face was thin and long and her nose accounted for a large part of her face. It was not broad and flaring, but it was straight and big and almost like that of a cartoon character. She had a cocoa-brown complexion with freckles staring out boldly from all over her face. Her brown feline eyes looked enquiringly from Slinky to Deidre-Ann.

She was forming a question on her lips when her eyes caught the blood on Deidre-Ann's hand. "Good Lord girl yuh bleeding, what is the matter? Slinky how did she get this cut, ah hope yuh not responsible for it!" Her voice trailed away as she reached for Deidre-Ann, not waiting for an answer. She put her to sit on a stool and went into another room.

Deidre-Ann closed her eyes. She was weakened by pain and the loss of blood. She felt dizzy and disoriented as she sat there trying to piece together the events of that day. What was she doing in this place and how had she got there? Slinky had left the room and she really wanted to ask her where she was, and how she could get back to civilization.

While she was submerged in thought, the lady came back into the room. "My name is Arnell Malcolm but everybody call me Miss Nellie. What is your name?"

Deidre-Ann did not answer. She did not really want to go telling people her name. Then an idea presented itself. She would make up a fictitious name, nobody really needed to know her real name. "My name is Kimola." She could not tax herself at the moment to find a surname.

Miss Nellie came around to her with a small basin of steaming hot water, some old bottles and jars, and what looked like bandage. "Ah going to dress the cut for yuh an' when mi finish yuh won't need any doctor at all, at all!"

Deidre-Ann grimaced as Miss Nellie wiped the cut clean with alcohol. For the first time, she saw the full extent of the injury. It was about two inches long and deep enough for one to see a little way down into it. In her mind, it needed stitches to close it. She would have to see to that tomorrow. Miss Nellie put some salt on the cut, and then a concoction which looked like beaten green leaves. She placed some gauze-looking material on top of the wound and then bandaged it. Deidre-Ann wondered where she had got all of this material from, but felt too pained and sleepy to question her.

Miss Nellie noticed the fatigue and said to her, "Yuh look as if yuh going to faint any minute now, come and lie down in here." She pointed to the room where she had disappeared earlier.

"Can I, can I use your bathroom?" Deidre-Ann asked feebly.

"Yes, come this way." She led her through the room to which she had gone earlier into a small bathroom which was about four feet by four. It contained an aging over-worked beige basin and toilet, and a concrete bathing area which had been scrubbed so often that the paint had refused to cover it. Deidre-Ann's main reason for going to the bathroom was to hide her money and ATM card. She remembered how the helper had told her family that she would not go into a particular area without hiding her money in her bra for safety, so Deidre-Ann used a piece of the plastic in which she had received the items she had bought, and wrapped the items in it and then tied it to her bra. She did not want to become a mendicant and furthermore she trusted no one. For all she knew, Slinky might very well had taken her up there to rob her. *If I have any sense*, she thought, *I should just go back and try to find the hotel, but who would take me there at this time of the night?*

The following morning, she woke up and jumped up, frightened. She wondered what day it was and where she was. It was daylight and the sun, uninvited, had invaded her privacy by peeping through the jalousies. She saw a form beside her and jumped, then she realized that she was not at home, but in Miss Nellie's bed. It was an old fashioned twin spring bed. Some of the springs had undone themselves and were trying to poke through the mattress. Deidre-Ann gazed around the room and saw a small square table with some crockery on it, an old fashioned dresser and a small, short what-not on which resided a tiny black and white television and an old radio. The ceiling was a dirty grey, with prominent water soaked patches which looked like nimbus clouds about to discharge rain.

A piercing tug of pain pulled her back to the reason she was in this strange place. She must get a bath and go back on the street so that she could find a suitable place to live. She got out of the bed and started searching for her belongings. As she bent down her head to pick up her bag, she experienced a paroxysm. It almost knocked her over and she sat on the floor, coughing. In addition to the pain in her hand, a persistent pricking started in her head. She blinked her eyes and uttered groans of pain, staying where she was.

It must have been the groans that awakened Miss Nellie. She sat up suddenly, looking around quizzically and then she got off the bed. There were not too many places to look in the small room so she soon located Deidre-Ann sitting on the floor, moaning with her head in her hand.

"Oh God lilly girl, what yuh doing down there? An' yuh must really be sick to be sitting there!" Her voice held sympathy and alarm. She got up and went over to Deidre-Ann to assist her and said in surprise, "Kimola, yuh burning up with feva, my God ah could roast anything on yuh!" She assisted her back to bed.

Deidre-Ann drifted in and out of pain, sleep and dizziness for the next two days. She knew that other people were in and out of the room but she took no note, they were only fuzzy, indistinct shadows hovering around and then disappearing.

# CHAPTER ELEVEN

## *Deidre-Ann's Ordeal Continues*

*I*t was two days later that Deidre-Ann started feeling like a human being. She still ached, but the pain was concentrated mainly in her arm which was bandaged with a piece of cloth. She wondered whose garment had been sacrificed in aid of medicine. She was wearing a large ill-fitting housedress that kept falling from her shoulders. Deidre-Ann clawed at it, horrified at the thought of wearing other people's clothes. In the same instance she remembered the money she had tied to her bra. She felt for it eagerly, hoping against hope that it had not been removed. Her heart dipped and started racing fiercely. The money was gone.

She catapulted out of the bed and called loudly, "Miss Nellie! Miss Nellie!" There was panic and anger in her voice.

Miss Nellie came running. "Miss Kimola, yuh feel betta, yuh want something, what's the matter now?" She looked anxious and horrified.

Without saying good morning, Deidre-Ann blurted out, "Where's my money that I had on me...where is it?"

"Oh," Miss Nellie said, relieved. "Ah taut yuh was in pain. T'ank God yuh feel better. Don't worry yuhself, yuh belongings safe. Ah put it up for yuh."

Deidre-Ann felt foolish, yet happy. "Thank you Miss Nellie. I was really distressed. I need to have it now cause I want to go away." As an after-thought, she added, "I thank you for helping me. I don't know what would have happened if you did not."

Before Miss Nellie could answer, the door was pushed open and three girls burst into the room without invitation. They stared at Deidre-Ann without speaking. "Mitzie, Linette and Carla, this is Kimola, you didn't get to meet her cause she been sick all the time. Somebody cut her hand an' it cause her to have feva." She looked at them, begging for words of sympathy.

Mitzie and Linette mumbled "Morning" and scrutinized Deidre-Ann carefully. The third one, Carla, looked at her and a frown appeared on her face.

She turned to Miss Nellie sourly, her black and blue curly wig shaking as she spoke. "Yuh nuh tired to tek in strays, how much more a dem yuh a go carry come park up on top a the other?" The bitterness in her voice was unbridled and deep-seated, especially when she looked at Deidre-Ann, who looked away from her in an effort to ward off the wicked glare.

"Don't pay mi granddaughter any mind," Miss Nellie said, trying to make light of the bitter verbal attack. "She always behave like that but her name deh at the altar of prayer an' one day she mus' yield to God an' change."

"Don't tell mi nothin' bout yuh an' yuh church an' prayer!" Carla snapped like an angry dog which wanted to devour an intruder. "If prayer coulda help yuh, how come yuh live here so inna so much poverty an' squalor? Tell me dat! Tell me dat!" The frustration and anger were almost choking her.

"T'ings would have been better if yuh neva live here an' rob me of what ah muss get." Miss Nellie looked at her and pursed her lips like a draw string bag. Her voice lacked the fire and anger which characterized her grand-daughter's, instead, schooled patience and tolerance came forth.

Deidre-Ann pitied her and decided that this was not the place for her. She watched the small sharp eyes as they raked the grandmother, getting ready to launch more missiles of accusations. Miss Nellie seemed to be accustomed to the assaults as she moved away from the unveiled venom and started tidying the room, bursting into a song, as she did so. "Rock of ages cleft for me, Let me hide myself in thee." Her voice held sad hope and spoke of pained perseverance.

Carla would not allow Miss Nellie to cover her problems in the comfort of the song, so she fired back. "What you expect me to do, ah was born in sin and shape in lust and savagery, in rape did my mother conceive me, an' in the slums of lust and poverty did my unrighteous-righteous grandmother raise me!"

The pointed missiles of words struck the grandmother and her singing stalled and spluttered then started again before slurring to a stop. She turned as if to reply and then turned away, her mouth opening and closing like a young bird yearning for food.

"What yuh all doing in here so?" a gruff voice asked.

Everybody turned to see Slinky in the room. True to his name, he had come in quietly without anyone hearing him.

"Slinky ah neva hear yuh, yuh move fast an' quiet like a cat," Miss Nellie commented.

Carla fixed him with a look of disapproval and then moved past him, almost pushing him aside.

Slinky hissed his teeth and then turned to Miss Nellie. "Ah bet she is here cussing you off again! She need to fine a new employment along with the one she already doing."

"Alright Slinky nuh bother with she. She can't do more than her time, one day she mus' stop unless my God dead!"

The two girls went out and as they did, Deidre-Ann noted their dress, coloured wigs, and shorts which struggled to cover their bottoms.

Slinky followed her gaze and commented, "My girl, roun' here yuh have to survive; when dem dress like dat, a little attraction come dem way an' a so dem survive."

Deidre-Ann did not want to find out what the little attraction was, she wanted to get out fast. She would try and find her way to her grand aunt who lived in the country. Maybe she could get her to keep her mouth shut and try to get her out of the country somehow.

"Miss, can I borrow your bathroom a little? This stray does not want to stay here and be a problem for your granddaughter or anyone. I need to freshen up and leave before it becomes too late."

"Leave, yuh caa leave here now!" Slinky walked urgently towards Deidre-Ann and lowered his voice. "Yuh caa go out dere now, danger is walking around!"

"What yuh mean?" asked Miss Nellie, moving towards Slinky and Deidre-Ann.

"Which danger, what do you mean?" Deidre-Ann asked, worry seeping into her voice.

"Dis morning when ah go out on the street news spread of 'bout how Belris cut you up and dere was a man there asking question 'bout yuh."

"Man? What kind of man? Policeman, family, who?" Deidre-Ann asked anxiously, leaning close to him, forgetting that he was a man and little more than a stranger.

"A man with a kind a grayish beard, an' him not that tall nor so short either. Is him yuh father or what?"

"No, even though I haven't seen him for years, that could not have made him any shorter. He is a big, tall man." She shook her head to emphasize her certainty.

"But him seh him is yuh father an' dat him really want to fine you and carry yuh back home. Him seh yuh is not a bad gal, jus' a little confused 'bout some t'ings. Him a offer money to anyone who can help him find yuh." Slinky was almost breathless as he related his findings.

"One thing is certain, that man, whoever he is, is not my father so I wonder why he's looking for me? I wonder if he's the man in charge of those with the special job, and as they said, I had no right on their corner and he wants to beat me up." Deidre-Ann spoke with a questioning tone, not knowing what to think.

"No sah! No way! Is not so the pimp dem work! Dem work under cover cause dem no want police fi sort dem out! No sah is not one a dem!" He was adamant about this because he was at home on the street and knew what went on there.

"Den is mus' somebody working for di police dem," Miss Nellie offered. "Maybe yuh mother or somebody sen' him out there to fine you. Dem really want yuh whoever dem sen' him!" She looked at Deidre-Ann in a strange way and it was clear she was wondering what her story was.

Deidre-Ann could both see and feel two pairs of eyes looking, questioning, probing, watching her intently with the hope that she would divulge some information, but she said nothing. It was not time to tell anyone about her past, especially when she would soon be moving on. As they stood there expectantly, there was a sound by the door as if something had fallen. Slinky rushed forward and flung the door open but saw nothing or no one. He closed back the door and stood listening with his ears glued to it and then he suddenly opened it again but saw no one. He went into the room and out through the door, but only saw Mitzie and Linette talking to the neighbours next door, Carla was nowhere in sight.

Slinky went back into the room. Miss Nellie and Deidre-Ann were still standing there silently.

"Ah have a strange feeling dat somebody was standing dere and listening. An' ah don't really want the girls to know what is happening to Kimola cause news could spread an' we don't want any trouble up here."

Slinky went away for the rest of the day and Deidre-Ann asked Miss Nellie what he did all day on the road.

"Well, Kimola, him clean windshield an' beg at the same time. Him can't read so good, only sign him name an' a few more words so him can't get no job."

"Is he related to you or what? How come he's living here with you?" Deidre-Ann's curiosity had got the better of her.

"Well is a long story, but the short of it is dat him mother abondan him an' him nuh have nuh father an' even though ah really neva have anything, ah still let him live with me from him was ten. Him neva go school often cause a di money problem, and him really nuh like school even though him have hole heap a sense, an' say him waan turn soldier. But mi no know how dat will ever happen because him nuh have nuh soul in the world to help him. Only God Almighty, would a bring such a miracle to pass." Her voice changed to a prayerful tone as if she was talking to God at the same time she was talking to Deidre-Ann.

"You know I could help him with the reading if he comes home early in the night, as I might be here for a few days until I know what's going on out on the street." It was a genuine offer though Deidre-Ann did not know why she made it, but he had helped her once and he was really trying to help her again, so she did not see why not, one good turn deserved another.

"Yuh can tell him when him come in tonight an' hear what him say. Miss Teeny daughter what live down the road did start up one night school an' him did go down dere two night, but him sey too much people down dere an' plus Carla laugh him to scorn an' tell him say dat a nuh everyting mek fi dog."

"But can she read?" Deidre-Ann wanted to know.

"Yes, good good, but she nuh waan put her head to not'ing except malice an' bitterness. She will spen' de res' of her days cussing her mother for bringing har into dis worl' an' not providing up town life fi she." Miss Nellie had clearly resigned herself to Carla and her ways.

"I am not staying here for long," Deidre-Ann said, reassuring both Miss Nellie and herself. "Carla really dislikes me and I really do not want to get in her way. As soon as the coast is clear, I am getting out of here."

"A t'ink yuh should go back home wherever dat is an' mek it up with your people. Ah don't know yuh story, but it clear from the way yuh talk dat you come from some up town place, down here so not going to help yuh at all." She looked at her once more and Deidre-Ann knew she was inviting her to talk about her situation and what had brought her there. She looked away, determined not to talk, the time was not right, neither were the people, and then some events were not clear in her mind. It could be that in her mind she was not trying hard enough to find the rapist. What was she afraid of?

During the day, she had a good chance to look at the community she was staying in. It was a low-income two bedroom, one bathroom housing scheme. The houses were semi-detached with a small space for additions at the side, if the owner could afford it. Miss Nellie had added on a plyboard room for Slinky and a small kitchen made of the same material. The room Deidre-Ann was sharing was Miss Nellie's and the other girls shared the other room. Deidre-Ann had learnt the same morning that Mitzie and Linette were her friends' daughters. Their mothers had gone to the USA when the girls were only twelve and had not been seen since. As Carla had suggested, Miss Nellie had 'collected' them. As a result of limited finances, they were in and out of school a little bit more frequently than public holidays and even though the blueprint for learning was present, they did not present themselves to be taught.

The houses were almost rubbing shoulders and one could hear the discussions, quarrels, laughs and everything else that involved human relationships. There were no driveways into these houses, so the few vehicles were parked along the narrow road, which had more holes than road and reminded Deidre-Ann of black and brown polka dot material.

Not wanting to be a burden, Deidre-Ann gave Miss Nellie some money for food. The only income she had was the small sum of money she received from Carla's mother, five maybe six times per year. Slinky did not contribute money, but sometimes brought home a few things to eat from his car washing occupation. He did not really eat at home, unless he had had a really bad day on the street. He came home about eight o'clock that night and Miss Nellie was more than surprised.

"Wait Slinky is what happen? Police chasing yuh or what? What yuh really doing here so early in the night?" Her surprise was evident as she walked over to his room.

"Miss Nellie ah always tell yuh, I am a street boy, but me not a wrongdoer! Ah hussle and beg, but ah don't t'ief an' a only fight with a man if him violate and want to fight me!" He was very empathetic with his declaration and Deidre-Ann felt the emphasis was meant for her.

"Slinky ah never say yuh was a wrongdoer, but yuh know that sometimes yuh don't have to do anything but fine yuhself on the road at the wrong time, at the wrong place, in the wrong clothes, an' in the wrong company an' look like yuh come from the wrong part of town, an' yuh is a goner." Her voice was filled with experience and sadness, the sadness of one who knew and had seen too much in one lifetime.

"Ah really come home early because too much not happening out there an' ah really have some hot news for Kimola! My girl yuh more popular than food! Not only man wid beard who yuh say is not your father out there looking for yuh, but de police out dere showing your picture an' asking everyone if dem see dis person!" His eyes looked wild with entertainment, thrilled at being the one to bring the news and expectant as he felt certain that Deidre-Ann would reveal something about her past, something that had placed her on everyone's most wanted list.

Deidre-Ann did not fulfill their expectancy; their thirst for her past was not about to be quenched. Instead she asked, "Where were they, at the park or where the girl cut me?"

"At de park but dat nuh very far from weh yuh get de knife. News travel faas an' mi hear dat the girl ah go shif' her spot cause she 'fraid police."

"How did you know that it was the police asking for me? How do you know it was not people pretending to be police? Were they wearing uniforms?" Deidre-Ann looked inquiringly at Slinky.

"No not uniform, plain clothes, but dem come inna police car an' dem have on ID. Dem also offering money to fine you! Kimola is what really happen, what yuh really do so?" His voice was filled with concern, not just wanting to hear her business.

"I am not a criminal, I just run away from home that's all," replied Deidre-Ann quietly without looking at any of them. She was not lying, just telling them something they already knew without providing the reasons.

"Ah guess dat long time," Miss Nellie answered. "Jus' like how ah guess yuh not the roun' here type a person. Everything bout yuh seh dat, yuh have education an' all dat, but something went wrong an' it mus' have been very bad, cause yuh pick up an' run wey. Ah hope dat they don't fine you up here, cause dem going to want to harass me, say ah harbor you. An'..."

Deidre-Ann interjected. "Don't bother Miss Nellie, I will be out of here in the next two days as soon as I make some phone calls and make some arrangements. I won't let any of you get into trouble."

"We not getting into trouble over anything! Miss Nellie don't frighten di girl! Is only us who live in here know dat she is here," he remonstrated, giving Miss Nellie a shocked look.

"Ah not running her out on the street or anyt'ing, yuh know ah would never do dat! Ah was only saying dat since so much people a look for her ah could get into trouble. Ah only want to help you Miss," she said turning to Kimola. "Ah only want to help you!" She was begging to be understood, begging to live up to her name of collecting troubled young people.

"I know and I appreciate your help, but I don't want to get you into trouble at all." Deidre-Ann clearly understood Miss Nellie's way of thinking.

To Miss Nellie's surprise, Slinky agreed to Deidre-Ann helping him, and the teaching started that very night. About an hour later, a vehicle pulled up at the gate and Slinky peeped through the window and made a sound of disgust. "Well dem two going now, late tonight or early tomorrow mawning before dem come back here!"

"Who you talking?" asked Deidre-Ann, going to the window. She needed no answer, because as she looked Linnette and Mitzie climbed into the comfort of a silver Honda Picnic.

"Do they do this all the time?" Deidre-Ann asked. "Where are they going?"

"Yuh wouldn't waan to fine out dat, put two an' two together an' four will jump out at you!" he said, turning away from the window. "Miss Poison soon gone to, she worse than dem two, different one every time!" Even though he was a man of the street, the stance with which he held such activity was fraught with derision and disdain. "That nite when yuh was out there a thought yuh was one of dem, but is after yuh get the cut an' ah look at yuh ah realize that yuh was the kind girl in the park. And moreover yuh never dress like dem either." He looked at her with respect and the harsh face softened a little.

Although Deidre-Ann saw the loosening of the tightness on Slinky's face, one could see the pique in her eyes. It still rankled that the taxi-driver and all those girls thought she was a part of that industry when she felt such loathing for the male gender and humans in particular who saw her as vermin or an object of pity. One day she would show them.

She continued to help Slinky by helping him to pronounce simple everyday words and then putting them in simple sentences that he could read. She found him to be an eager student, and found out that he knew more than the few words that Miss Nellie thought he knew.

When she was about to end her lesson, a vehicle purred to a stop at the gate. As Carla, who must have been awaiting its arrival, flashed open the gate, a man stepped out of the SUV. The two peering through the window thought he was going to meet her but instead he bent down as if to examine his front left tyre. As he stood up with his back turned to the house, Deidre-Ann felt that there was something familiar about him. It was weird that this feeling should come over her, but the feeling was very strong. She wondered where and how, and would have liked to see his face but he kept his back turned even as he went back into the vehicle without going over to the passenger side to open the door for Carla. He drove off softly for such a big vehicle. The engine was evidently well tuned and serviced.

For the next few days, Deidre-Ann kept herself out of the sight of her prying neighbours. They had obviously heard that there was a new girl in Miss Nellie's collection, and were anxious to see what she looked like. They came knocking at Miss Nellie's front door to ask her questions about any and everything, especially about remedies for sickness and pain and also to beg or borrow food items: a piece of butter, a little oil in a cup, a cup of rice, a little salt. Deidre-Ann's eyes grew rounder and rounder every time the items were announced. She knew that poverty existed but she had no idea that people who were not living on the street were this poor.

The begging and seeking of advice were accompanied by peeping over Miss Nellie's shoulder to get a glimpse of the new girl, whom they heard was sick so she had not hit the street yet. This was one of the stories spread by Carla according to Slinky. Deidre-Ann knew what they were trying to do so she kept way out of their line of vision. Some of the neighbours, although they were often begging, cursed Miss Nellie as soon as they were out of her presence.

"Ah don't understand how a woman like dis who claim seh she a Christian could a have so much a dem kine a gal roun' her." The woman who spoke put down the cup of rice she had just begged on the neighbour's wall.

"It look like seh she nuh read de word of God to dem and pray fi dem like odda people! Three gal who live a road when night come and a good fi nutten boy who live on the street! Parson need to read her out a de church!" Her neighbour bent over her gate and fixed her head tie as she joined in the assault.

"It really look bad an' me hear seh, annada gal inside a hide, mi don't know how true it is!" a third one informed, glaring at Miss Nellie's house as if willing the answer to appear.

Miss Nellie was not oblivious of the gossip and she did what she had always done, took it to God on her knees. Deidre-Ann had an idea what was being said because the houses almost rubbed shoulders with one another and the voices were loud and sharp. She secretly planned to leave because Slinky had not mentioned anything about her pursuers in two days. She wanted to leave in the wee hours of the morning to avoid the people, but the community in which she was never slept, there were people on the street at all times, day and night. She shuddered as she thought of falling into the wrong hands; this had to be avoided at all cost. If that ever happened to her again she knew what she would have to do, if he or they did not do it to her. She would have to work with Slinky in this one.

She was becoming more uncomfortable with Carla. She exhibited open hostility towards her, and often sought to engage her in quarrels for no apparent reason. Sometimes she would just burst open Miss Nellie's room without invitation and fix Deidre-Ann with an ugly glare without saying a word and then she would laugh like a hyena and disappear. Deidre-Ann wondered what secret she was harbouring. She was sure that she was up to something sinister.

Deidre-Ann was also experiencing something new. It would not have been truthful to say that the household she was coming from was not a godly one, but Miss Nellie was something different. She would, without warning, place her hand on Deidre-Ann and pray for her. Deidre-Ann did not resist or resent the prayer even though she was not accustomed to the down to earth, emotional talking to God as if he were an earthly companion. She somehow made praying and God more real and awesome at the same time. She also read the Bible to Deidre-Ann in her halting, careful voice. She encouraged her to read it daily for herself, because she was certain that God could help her with whatever problems she was having and put her life back on track.

During her second week, she surprised herself and went to church with her on Sunday. Of course, Carla stood at the gate and laughed herself into a coughing fit punctuated by hiccups. Deidre-Ann knew that she was not attired as she would have been back home but she went none the less, comforting herself with the idea that it was a church right there in the community and people would not overdress. She was wrong about this, hats matched shoes, dresses and handbags and some of the men were attired in ties and suits, some large and ill-fitting.

Deidre-Ann knew that she would be stared at, asked questions and whispered about, so she braced herself. That day, Miss Nellie had more greetings than ever before, greetings which ended with long stares and pointed questioning. "Ah see yuh get a new girl, is yuh relative or what?"

"What a pretty girl, what is her name?"

"Ah glad this girl interested in church! Invite her back again!"

Deidre-Ann endured it all, but she didn't mind the vibrant service in which the pastor promised hellfire for all sinners. He spent a long time naming and emphasizing the sins, amidst loud amens, hallelujahs and tongues. When he mentioned prostitution, some heads turned in Deidre-Ann's direction. She was truly horrified that the people thought that she was a prostitute. It was only Miss Nellie's firm, straining hand on hers that kept her from walking out. She vowed never to return and to leave the community as quickly as possible. It seemed as if she had no place in the world. At one end she was a rape victim to be scorned and pitied, and at the other, a prostitute in need of help!

She walked home in quiet anger, not paying much attention to the stares or Miss Nellie's words of comfort. She had lost everything, why should she go on living? The salt had lost its savour and was therefore not good enough for anything, not even existing. As if to deepen her depression, Slinky came home with news that the bearded man was again on the prowl and so were the police. This news frustrated Deidre-Ann. She was in a spin, which way was she to turn? She wondered if Slinky was fabricating lies in order to keep her there, but when she asked him outright, he was outraged and said he only lied for convenience and not about serious things.

Miss Nellie, on hearing this, encouraged Deidre-Ann to go back home and work things out with her people, because she was certain that the bearded man was up to no good and would seriously hurt her if he laid hands on her.

Deidre-Ann did something that night that she had not done since leaving home. She called her home. There was no answer at the first call, the phone just kept on ringing until the answering machine chipped in. She called again although she was not certain why, since she didn't want to speak to anyone. She had started feeling guilty about putting them through the agony that she knew they were experiencing. When a voice answered, she jumped, frightened to hear her sister's voice at the other end.

"Hello, hello," the voice repeated hesitantly, warily.

Deidre-Ann did not answer. Her heart did a sprint race instead.

Her sister got angry and screamed into the phone, "So now you are up to playing tricks! Why don't you just give your usual threats and get off the phone!" She stopped for a while and listened, but no one answered. The fury in her voice lashed out at Deidre-Ann on the other end. "So you have run out of threats, but guess what, yes we are still alive! We live here and even though you have wrecked Deidre-Ann's life, I am not allowing you to wreck anyone else's. So come up here and get me, you know where I live, rapist!"

Deidre-Ann flinched as the phone clattered on the other side. She sat dazed and stared stupidly at the wall in front of her as if she expected the answer to the question forming in her mind to appear on it. One had appeared for Nebuchadnezzar who had fallen from grace, why shouldn't one appear for her who had fallen from humanity? She tried to put some kind of sense to her sister's response to her silent call. Apparently someone had been calling her home and making threats which were related to what had happened to her. She was not the only one in danger, her family was too! Was the person afraid that she could identify him and was threatening the family to keep her silent? Did he intend to do the same thing to her sister if he could not find her? The whirlwind of questions swirled around in her head and made her giddy with fear. It didn't matter what Slinky said, she had to leave the community before word seeped out about her whereabouts.

Miss Nellie had gone to church and only Carla was in the other room. The other two girls had gone to a dance down the street and Slinky had not arrived home as yet. The room was hot and she sat by the only window in the room and opened it a little to allow fresh air to steal inside. She stared out at the houses across the street. There was not much movement in them or on the street; it seemed as if most people had gone to the dance. She could hear the music screaming irritably into the night air. She heard a sound around the side of the house and spun around quickly. It was Carla going to the dance. As she passed by the window, Deidre-Ann's eyes and mouth opened like a fish gulping for air. Carla was wearing one of her few dresses! She knew that a world war would begin if she said anything to her, but she couldn't just sit and let her go.

"Carla, that's my dress you are wearing! I did not give you permission to do such a thing!" She opened the window wider and pushed her head outside.

"Sure is your dress, but come an' tek it off me if yuh bad!" Carla stood arms akimbo as if waiting for Deidre-Ann to come outside.

Deidre-Ann felt the anger building inside her. She withdrew her head and took a step towards the door, then stopped. She didn't want to fight with Carla, that was not her style. She would not drag herself down into the gutter anymore. She went back to the window and looked calmly at Clara who laughed and shouted, "Yuh turn back coward! Yuh should come out and let me finish you off before..." She stopped and laughed again, enjoying her own secret joke. "Ah soon fix yuh business good and proper! Ah behave like yuh nice!" She flounced off in the direction of the dance, wiggling her narrow frame and laughing.

The laughter irked Deidre-Ann, of all the things she hated about Carla, her heinous hyena-laughter supplanted all. She was already bordering on hysteria and the un-nerving laughter caused her body to tremble a little.

She was about to close the window when an SUV crept to a stop at the gate. It was the same one that had come to pick up Carla a few days earlier. It waited for a minute and when no one went out to meet it, it started tooting its horn. It didn't sound that loud because of the blaring music coming from down the street. The driver must have realized that he was competing with the music, or maybe he had become impatient, so he opened the door slowly, got out and walked towards the gate. He opened it and came towards the front door. As Deidre-Ann watched, the feeling of familiarity rushed over her again. She leaned forward out of the window to see a little better.

The man must have seen the open window and the person looking out because he came towards the window. He stopped when he was a few feet away and asked in a sonorous voice, "Is Carla inside? Can you ..." his voice died away and he peered closer at Deidre-Ann, who was peering at his features which were illuminated by the light from the light post which stood only a few feet from the house. He had stopped speaking and was staring too. They both stared, each looking foolishly at the other. Deidre-Ann could stare no longer and she slumped to the floor in a dead faint.

Slinky dashed to his house as if he were being chased by hounds. He didn't slink in as he usually did. He pounded on Miss Nellie's door and almost forgot to wait for an answer. He was getting ready to turn the lock when he heard a faraway, faint unintelligible sound. He turned the lock forcefully and a screw fell out. He paid no attention to the damage and bumped into Miss Nellie's table, sending a glass clattering to the floor. "Miss Nellie, weh yuh deh? Stop praying now!" He heard another sound and went towards it. He saw Deidre-Ann sitting on the floor. "What yuh doing down there? Get yuh t'ings quickly, we haffi leave right now!"

Deidre-Ann was sitting on the floor with her head in her hands. She had hit her head when she fainted and had lain there for a while before she regained consciousness. She sat on the floor trying to concentrate on the pain in order to get the bewildered feeling out of her mind.

"Hurry Kimola you have to leave now! Trouble a come right now! Jus' grab yuh bag an' come!" He was highly agitated and the urgency caused his voice to tremble. He pulled her up from the floor and as soon as she located her bags, he took them from her and pulled her along unceremoniously. He led her through his room, locked it behind him and went out on the street. They were two lamp-posts from the house when he whispered,

"Jesus Father!" and pulled her through the open gate of the closest house and told her to bend behind the wall. She did not hesitate or question him but complied.

She heard low voices and hurried footsteps pass on the other side of the wall. Without knowing why, goose bumps and sweat rushed to the surface of her skin. She was bending close to a plant which had an unpleasant smell and a sneeze started straining to be released but she pushed her hand into her mouth and bit down hard and it relented.

At the same time Slinky whispered, "Get up slow an' look quick!"

"Look where?" she whispered, looking in all directions.

"Look at the house!" he snapped back impatiently.

The same light which had illuminated the face of the man as he spoke to her by the window shone fully on Carla and a bearded man as they opened the door to Miss Nellie's house! She gave a frightened gasp and Slinky touched her hand to prevent any movement.

They watched as the two entered the house, then Slinky quietly opened the gate and half dragged Deidre-Ann down the street.

# CHAPTER TWELVE

## Clues Are Followed

Nathan got out of the car and knocked on Mrs. Lenworth's gate. He looked at his watch and noted that it was almost one o' clock. He was surprised that the sun was behaving in such a friendly manner that day. Its usual fierceness had been replaced by the smiles which faded in and out. A few clouds drifted by lazily, stopping frequently to hail other clouds which were sauntering in the coolness of the early afternoon.

He knocked at the gate again. A 'coming!' from inside was also accompanied by a deep growl from the dog next door. Annoyed at having its rest disturbed, it growled its way to the front and looked at Nathan in an unfriendly manner. Nathan ignored it and focused on the house in front of him. He observed that the usual tidy lawn had several patches of defiant weeds asserting themselves above the legitimate plants. The plants at the hedge were now crowding over the wall, and the shapes of the usually well trimmed trees had become shabby and undefined. He glanced at the gardens and plants close by and noticed that they had maintained the status quo of the community. He had sent a gardener over but it appeared as if he had come only once.

The front door creaked opened and Ashley appeared at the grill with the key in her hand. She had been expecting Nathan so she did not cast furtive glances around as she usually did since Deidre-Ann's ordeal. Nathan noticed the jaded, lackluster features of the young woman who should have been reflecting the rosy hue of youth. He reminded her of a flower which had been stunted before the petals could gain full colour, having been battered by the unthinking elements. He hoped that he could bring some kind of closure to this case soon and that he could help to inject some measure of life back into the family.

He hugged her when she opened the grill. He could feel the tenseness and fear which were locked inside her. Mrs. Lenworth was sitting in an armchair watching them as they came through the door. Nathan pushed back the lump which formed without warning in his throat. To say that she looked forlorn was an understatement. He wondered how long she could really hold out before her nerves caved in completely. The graying hair which once outlined her forehead had bred by bounds and had now invaded much of her hair. The eyes had become dead and heavy and the lines at the corner of her mouth had dug deeper into her skin. Nathan estimated that she had lost over twenty pounds. The sleeveless dress she was wearing sagged like a deflating balloon when she got up to greet him.

"You don't have to get up." He waved her back down, swallowing yet another lump which was determined to choke him. She didn't sit so he steered her over to the sofa so he could sit beside her. Ashley came in with glasses of iced tea, passed them around and then slumped into an armchair.

Nathan sipped his drink and then rested it on the lamp table beside him. He cleared his throat, gave a hint of smile and started. "The reason why I came up here today is that I have a little information that might give us some hope." He stopped and took another sip from his drink. Mrs. Lenworth and Ashley leaned forward, a glint of expectation creeping into their faces. Nathan continued. "The first day that Ann left here she was seen at the park."

"Who saw her and what was she doing?" Mrs. Lenworth asked, sitting upright suddenly, upsetting the seat.

"Take it easy, I don't mean to give you false hope. She was seen in the park and our lead says she was involved in an incident with some girls of the dark and she might have got hurt. She has disappeared into nothingness because she has never been seen again. However..."

"Never been seen, so for all we know she might be dead and gone! It's better you never say anything at all!" This came from Ashley whose face had become darkened with sorrow. She slumped back in the armchair, her feet visibly shaking.

"If only I had not sent her back to school!" Mrs. Lenworth wailed. "She would be alive now!"

"Listen, I didn't say she was dead. I just said she has not been seen since. We ..."

"Has not been seen since, euphemism for dead! Involved in an incident with girls of the dark, euphemism for beaten, injured or killed!" Ashley's voice rose to a crescendo and hovered there. "Poor Ann, God what did she do to deserve this, so young, so much promise, so innocent!"

"Come now..." Nathan held Mrs. Lenworth's hand. "We are following a lead and if you give me a chance, I will explain." He paused and looked at Mrs. Lenworth. She made a groan and Nathan took that as an agreement to go ahead. "Do you remember the bearded man who went to Ann's school posing as her father?" A nod from his two relatives was enough for him to continue. "He has been on the street asking questions about Ann. We have also learnt that he is offering a reward to anyone who can lead him to her. He is still claiming to be her father and behaves as if he is smitten with grief."

"Why don't you arrest and question him?" Mrs. Lenworth asked, disbelief forming in her eyes. "I can't believe you have not at least questioned him!"

"Listen, listen," Nathan waved his hand in an attempt to be heard. "We are not going to arrest him or question him yet as we are hoping that he will lead us to Deidre-Ann. One of our men is disguised as a street boy and is following him. The reward he has offered is getting him attention. It seems as if one of the girls on the street is working with him. Our men trailed him into one of those low-income housing areas. We were certain that the girl was leading him to her but when they got to the place, she did not come out with him. If she was there she got wind of what was happening and left. We believe that there is someone working with her, helping her out, because as we all know Ann has never been anywhere by herself except school. We are watching the man every step of the way and something has to give. We believe he is working for someone as he is always on his phone talking to someone. We do not want him to know that we are on to him yet."

He got up suddenly and walked towards the kitchen, still talking. "I think he is going to bring some food to the station for us tomorrow." Mrs. Lenworth and Ashley looked at one another confused, that last statement of Nathan's did not make sense and why was he going towards the kitchen instead of asking them to get what he wanted?

Nathan walked to the kitchen door and turned left sharply. The frightened helper hiding behind the wall with her ears pressed to the wall and holding her work bag tightly, was so frightened that she could only look at Nathan with her mouth open and her eyes looking as if they were about to desert the sockets.

Nathan held her by the shoulders and steered her into the living room. "Now Elsie, could you please tell us why you were hiding and listening to our conversation?"

"Ah was coming from the dressmaker that Miss Lenny sen' me an' ah hear the voices an' peep in." As she sought to explain, the scowl on her face deepened into outrage.

"I have been watching you from this window and you stopped and spoke to a lady across the road, pointing to the house as you spoke to her. What were you pointing at?" Nathan looked into her eyes and held her gaze, willing her to answer.

"You police people t'ink that you are God. Since when it become illegal to talk and point to a house especially the one where I been working at for two years?" She appeared to be greatly taken aback.

"Now Elsie," Mrs. Lenworth intervened, "don't pass your place and be rude! You know we are in the middle of a problem and the police can ask questions about anything that they want to."

"Miss Lenny, what me have to do with Ann get missing, that any police would want to talk to me?" She looked at Mrs. Lenworth, begging for an answer.

"Elsie nobody said you were involved in anything. Nathan was just questioning why you were pointing at the house and why you were hiding and eavesdropping." She looked at the helper, hoping she would understand Nathan's motive.

"Eve dropping Miss! I not Eve and I never drop anything. What new crime is that that you want to say I do?"

Despite the situation, Ashley had to force back the laughter, eavesdropping a new crime! Elsie was really a comic.

"I really don't have the time to dabble in foolishness, If you have something to do go and do it." His dismissive tone further annoyed Elsie who walked off, looking back at him rudely.

Nathan went after her to see that she had left the kitchen area. When he got back he said to his two relatives, "There is something about her that always set me on edge. Every time I come up here I get the impression that she is watching, peeping and listening to everything we are saying. I was watching her through the window. Did you leave the back door open?" Nathan asked with a hint of disapproval in his voice.

"When you knocked at the gate, I remembered she was out and would soon come in so I called her and told her that the door was open," Mrs. Lenworth explained.

"You have to be careful of her, some things are not right but when I have worked it all out, I will tell you." He rose to go. "I have to leave now."

He walked to the door and the ladies accompanied him all the way to the car.

As they got to the car, a black Honda SUV drove up and turned at the neighbours' gate. A tall copper coloured man got out, leaving the door open. After he opened the door, he turned around.

"Oh it's Mr. Gayle," said Ashley. "I have not seen him since last year. I wonder how come he's here at this time."

"Mr. Gayle! Mr. Gayle!" Mrs. Lenworth called out. On hearing his name, Mr. Gayle waved to them and would have got back into the SUV, but Mrs. Lenworth stopped him. "Mr. Gayle are you in such a hurry that you can't say hello to your neighbour that you have not seen since last year?"

"Oh Mrs. Lenny it's not that, I have to get back to an important meeting in town but I suppose I can spend two minutes." He looked at his gold watch and wiped his face with a rag as she moved closer to him.

Nathan wondered why he was sweating so much since the sun was still on its mid siesta break and a cool wind was frolicking with the plants. Nathan watched him as he came forward. He had never seen him before. His forehead had sloped backwards with his slightly graying hair, which refused to cover his whole head and avoided the middle of it as if it were quicksand or a danger zone. His eyes were brown and slanted and did not settle down to look anyone directly into the eyes. His nose started out in a peak but ended up in waves which hovered over his thin turned-down mouth. Nathan wondered if he had a fever because he was sweating copiously and wiping the sweat with an almost sodden rag.

"Mr. Gayle, I thought you had left this island for good!" Mrs. Lenworth greeted him, proffering her right hand. He grasped it with his huge, hairy right hand. It was more like Mrs. Lenworth's hand being trapped into a huge animal's paw. She quickly extricated it.

"It's not that I don't come around but it's only now and then and when I come, you people not around. How is everyone and where is your next daughter? She must have graduated by now. I haven't seen her in a long while." His busy eyes flitted around. "And you Ashley, how is university treating you?"

"Fine, fine," said Ashley. "I will be out of there soon. Ann is not here right now."

"Well I have to go," he looked at his watch again and wiped his face.

"This is my cousin, Nathan," Mrs. Lenworth said as he turned to leave. "I don't think you have met him."

"Glad to meet you," he said, nodding at Nathan.

"Glad to meet you too," Nathan said, also nodding.

Mr. Gayle walked back to his SUV and got in while the three turned away.

Nathan, who was bringing up the rear, turned to look at him. As he did, he noticed that he had dropped his rag. He picked it up and opened his mouth to call to him but he had already started the SUV and could not hear him. Nathan shrugged his shoulders and after bidding his relatives goodbye and promising to call soon, he got into his car, still holding the rag.

# CHAPTER THIRTEEN

# Mr. Lenworth Turns Up

"Come in," Nathan said, not looking up from the sheet of paper he was busily writing on. His eyes were bright and his fingers seemed to write with a will of their own.

The door creaked open and a constable pushed his head into the room. "Sir, there's a man out here to see you, he said it was urgent."

"Ask one of the senior officers to deal with him cause right now I just can't. I'm into something deep here." He bowed his head over his paper and continued writing. He made pleasing sounds as he wrote.

There was a knock and again the door creaked open. "Sir, the gentleman refuse to talk to anyone else. He refuse to leave, said it is a matter of life and death and that no one else can deal with the problem except you. He said he is not leaving until you see him." The constable's voice contained the man's urgency. He was leaning against the door waiting for Nathan's response.

"What is his name?" Nathan asked, looking up from his paper.

"That is strange because he does not want to give his name, said you will know him when you see him."

The last statement got Nathan's attention. He covered the paper with the newspaper on his desk, sighed irritably and then said, "Send him in and whoever he is he had better have a good reason for disturbing me on this important morning." He changed the position of his chair and waited.

The door was closed and then it was opened again. The constable pushed his head around the door and announced, "Sir, here is the gentleman!"

Nathan stood up abruptly, upsetting the chair. For a while he just stared at the mortal specter before him. "You! You!" Nathan was experiencing a new dimension to his life, that of being at a loss for words. It was all he could do, summon something that was stronger than the physical will not to hit the man.

"I can identify with your shock but in the circumstance there is no one I feel that I turn to but you for help," said Mr. Lenworth, pulling out a chair and sitting without being told to. His frame was a close fit for the chair, but he sat and looked across at Nathan hopefully. His oblong hand-some face was serious and had a shame-faced quality about it. Nathan noticed the dark circles beneath his bleary red eyes. His hair was not as well combed as it ought to have been and he needed a shave, but these did not detract from his attractiveness. Nathan looked at him sitting there and saw a bit of Deidre-Ann and Ashley staring back at him. Despite his behaviour, he had never asked his cousin what she had seen in him. His debonair manner which Deidre-Ann had inherited had been a part of the fatal attraction and had also been a magnet for the willing females who had fallen for his allure and deception.

"After disappearing for so many years and not even trying to see your children once, where have you suddenly come from?" Nathan's voice had a nasty, pointed tone.

Mr. Lenworth winced visibly and the remorseful look on his face deepened. "After the constant quarrels and then that big finale, I thought it was better to keep my distance from everyone. I…"

"Including the two children you helped to bring into this world?" Nathan was not about to spare Mr. Lenworth's feelings.

"I know how it looks but my wife made it clear that I was not supposed to go anywhere near them." He was leaning forward in the chair, begging to be understood.

"I wonder who in the world could stop me from seeing my children! I have two before I got married and I visit them when I can at school, when they go to spend holiday with their grandparents and even at church! I have to know what is happening to them. You were just seeking an excuse. Womanizing should never stop you from seeing your children! You could even call them; you know them have a thing name cell phone!" He picked up his cell phone from the table and dangled it in front of Mr. Lenworth.

"I didn't call or visit but sometimes I get information about them." He looked at Nathan, hoping to score a point.

"Get information from who, when, except for the little money you send, nobody knows if you alive or dead! Get information from who?" Nathan was beside himself with anger.

"Mr. Gayle, Mr. Gayle next door always tell me what is going on. T..."

"Mr. who? You mean your neighbour who don't even seem to be around long enough to even say hello to his own family. Mr. Gayle! Tell me something, when last you talk to that man? When last you see him?" Nathan was now leaning forward towards Mr. Lenworth. His neck stretched to elastic proportion, and seemed likely to snap at anytime.

"What you so surprised about when I said Mr. Gayle? Him live next door and when I was living there, we always talk good. I wouldn't say we were close friends but we always got along well enough. The children use to visit his house now and again and him always seems to like them. I..."

"When last you talk to him? When last you see him?" Nathan's questioning was relentless, it was as if Mr. Lenworth was a suspect in a criminal case.

"Sometime last year, ah really don't remember when. When I call his house, they say he is not there and his cell phone always go to voice mail. I don't understand at all." There was undisguised confusion written all over his face. "Is he sick or dead or something?

Nathan ignored the inquiry. "Did he tell you what had happened to your daughter?" His tone had become soft, low, probing.

"Happen? Happen to which daughter? What you mean?" Mr. Lenworth was now standing and facing Nathan.

"Sit down, you look pathetic!" Nathan's voice had gone to a thunderous roar. "If you had been around then maybe things would have been different today!" Nathan accused, swiveling in his chair. It was just too much to sit still and face this man.

Unexpectedly, Mr. Lenworth sat. He was quiet for a while and Nathan could not be sure but he saw something which looked like a teardrop. "So you know what I am talking about?" Nathan's voice had again dropped, this time to a little above a whisper.

"Did something really bad happen to Ann?" Mr. Lenworth asked hesitantly. The words were having a problem coming out of his mouth. It was as if something was pushing them out reluctantly, forcefully.

"Why do you say it is Ann?" Nathan's voice was hoarse with emotion.

Mr. Lenworth held his face in his hands and shook his head slowly. Nathan was not sure what was happening and looked across dubiously at him. He called his name twice and when he got no response, he went over to him and shook him. The big man did not respond and Nathan impulsively flung his hands from his face in frustration.

"So you crying, is it shame or what? It's too late for that! Pull yourself together and face the problem like a big man!' Nathan was not about to issue false sympathy, especially not to someone so undeserving. "Pull yourself together and face things like a big man!"

209

The last few words must have wounded him because he looked up at Nathan as steadily as he could, the scathing insult from his words further deepening the remorseful look. Nathan moved away from him, it was not his forte to deal with emotionally crumbling men.

"It's because of Ann why I came to you," Mr. Lenworth began, unsure of how to put his misery into words. "I saw her and ..."

"You did what?" Nathan was again beside him. "You saw Ann? Where is she? How did you find her?"

"I didn't say I had found her! I said I saw her!" Mr. Lenworth emphasized.

"Stop fooling around and tell me what you meant!" Nathan shouted. "Have you found her or not!"

"If you calm down I might be able to explain!" Mr. Lenworth shouted back at him. "Give me a chance to explain myself!" He was standing and facing Nathan.

"I came to you because I saw my daughter somewhere she should have never been. The whole thing was so shocking that I can't come to terms with it!" He sat down again, bowed his head and groaned. Remembering Nathan's insult about behaving like a man, he raised his head and continued. "I went on a move, you know, to pick up a little girl..."

"Boy, after all these years you still a run down the little gal dem. Ah hope one day you land in a prison!" The scorn was evident in his voice.

"I am not proud of myself but God knows I am cured from this, no more young girl, no more running around after what could have happened!"

"Get on with the story, you make my stomach flip!" Nathan turned up his nose at him.

"When I went to this place to pick up the girl, she was not there. I walked over to her house to look for her and came face to face with my own daughter! My own daughter in a house reputed for harbouring prostitutes!" He groaned in mental torment.

"Ann, you saw Ann in a prostitute house? That could not be! Ann is not that type of girl. My guess is that she was hiding out at wherever you saw her!'

"Hiding out? Why would she be hiding out? What was she doing away from her mother and sister, away from her home?" He was clearly confused and concerned.

"When a man decides to neglect his legitimate children because of breaking up with his wife, he has no right to be asking such questions!" Nathan spoke into his face. He thought for a while and then he said, "Mr. Gayle obviously forget to give you the important details in T*he Days of My Absence*." He mockingly changed the words of the title of a popular story and made a flourish with his hand. He then very solemnly filled Mr. Lenworth in with all the sordid details of his daughter's ordeal.

It was pitiful to see how the grown man fell apart. Nathan almost withdrew his policy of giving sympathy to grown undeserving men. Mr. Lenworth sat for about five minutes before he could speak. Nathan did not interfere with him. He let him stay there and stew in his own sorrow. He deserved it for treating his children like scraps.

After he had given him what he thought was enough time to assimilate the details, he asked, "Did you say anything to her when you saw her?"

"No, I was so shocked. While I was staring she just disappeared from the window and I don't know how I got back to my vehicle, but I did. I went back to look for her the next day but she was gone just like how she disappeared the night before. Everyone in the house claimed ignorance about her whereabouts, but I think Carla and that street boy who lives at the house are involved. The boy, Slinky they call him, has disappeared also and I got his number from Carla but he's not answering at all."

"Well if I find him, I think we can find Ann, and most importantly, I am positive I know who the rapist is."

"Really! You really know?" Mr. Lenworth was standing up and for the first time that day, a smile appeared on his face.

"I know who he is but we are waiting on the DNA results and even before it comes we are trying to nab him. I am so excited about this. I need some information from you and I think there is somebody you should meet. I am going to arrange something."

"I hope when all this is over you will revise the way you have been living. What if you never remember what your own daughter look like and went out with her?" Nathan added, giving Mr. Lenworth a dirty look.

"The same thing occurred to me and that is why I will never go that way again."

"It's strange how some of us men behave. We do not see anything wrong with some of the things we do until family members or even our children become personally involved. It really is sad."

# CHAPTER FOURTEEN

## *Showdown, The Demons Are Slayed*

*D*eidre-Ann took out her phone and answered it. "Hello, hello. I can't hear you very well, you will have to shout because the music is loud and everyone is making noise."

"Deidre-Ann this is Mrs. Monroe, can you meet me in the car park, I need you to give me some information about the musicians who are playing." The voice sounded distant and a little coarse but Deidre-Ann attributed it to the noises incorporated with the loud music.

"Mrs. Munroe where are you parked? I need to find you quickly so that I can come back and finish taking care of things here," Deidre-Ann said, moving away from the music and shouting into the phone.

"You know my silver Mazda right? It is parked at the back of the Industrial Arts building. I had to park there because when I went on the road a little while ago, somebody took my usual parking spot. Hurry up because my son is supposed to come back and meet me here and

I don't want to move from here so that he can't find me."
With that Mrs. Munroe hung up.

"Marla I will be back shortly, Mrs. Munroe has called
me again. I have to give her some information." She hurried
outside, stopping a few times to greet several people.
She made her way to the back of the industrial arts
building. It was a little dark and no one seemed to be
around there. Deidre-Ann moved around, trying to see if
she could spot the car, calling out to Mrs. Munroe at the
same time. She got no response and was about to turn
back when huge, rough, dirty hands grabbed her. She
made a frightened little sound and put up her hands to
ward off the person. At first she could not see his face,
only two eyes peering at her. She freed one of her hands
and tried to gouge out the eyes in front of her. Her hand
came into contact with clothing and she pulled fiercely
at it. Her assailant grabbed at the cloth and they tugged
at it for a while. There was a tearing sound and even
though there was very little light, Deidre-Ann stared
into a familiar face.

"You, what are you doing?" she asked in horror. Without speaking, the assailant regained his ground and hit
Deidre-Ann once, then twice across the face. She grunted
and collapsed against him.

Deidre-Ann woke up screaming loudly. She thrashed
and kicked and then screamed again. "Let me go! What
are you doing?"

The room door was flung open and Mrs. Lindsay and
her daughter, Soliel, rushed in.

"Ann, for heaven's sake, what is wrong? Are you sick? Ann please stop screaming and tell us what's wrong." Mrs. Lindsay climbed on to the bed and held her hand. Soliel did the same.

"All right, we are here, don't worry," Soliel said, trying to calm the struggling girl.

"Aunt Lin, I know who did it! I know! I know!" She burst into fresh tears and kept on struggling. "I know who did it."

"Alright dear, calm down and tell me about it." She spoke softly, slowly, as if she was talking to a child.

Deidre-Ann stopped struggling and loud searing sobs shook her body. The two hugged her until they subsided somewhat.

"I knew something terrible was wrong when you showed up with that strange character and begged me not to call your mother until you had sorted out yourself. I cannot keep you here for too long without at least calling her or my brother. But Ann, dear, can't you just talk to us and tell us what is wrong so that we can help you?" her aunt pleaded, hugging her closer.

"Yes Ann, we will not tell anyone," her twenty-five year old cousin added.

Deidre-Ann lay where she was without moving, the only sounds were moans of distress that came at short intervals. Her aunt and her cousin continued to hold and comfort her. They thought she had fallen asleep, but five minutes later she sat up as if she had come to an agreement with herself and told them all she had been through, but she did not reveal the name of her attacker, except to tell them it had just come to her when everything was played back in a dream just now.

Her relatives were in tears and could hardly speak. It was only a little while after that her aunt said, "Sometimes the mind blots out trauma and only when we are ready to face up to something does it reveal everything. I cannot tell you how deeply affected I am by what has happened to you. I would not wish such an evil upon my worst enemy even if she were deserving. No one has any right to violate a woman in this way. It simply tugs one's heart out of place, but guess what, you cannot afford to let this evil dominate your life or stop you from being a whole human being. You have not done anything wrong, despite what the society we live in wants us to believe. How can someone take another person's integrity and passion for life away and that person ends up being the perpetrator instead of the victim?" She shook her head sadly and the tears continued on their course. "Guess what Ann, after we have contacted your mother and father, you can always live with us. There is more than enough space and I need company when Soliel goes away to study."

"Father?" Deidre-Ann sat up straight. "I do not want to have anything to do with that man. He is no better than the person who destroyed me!"

"That's another thing you have to learn, to forgive. I will not sit here and pretend for one fraction of a second that I would think or do anything differently from what you are thinking or doing, but I have to point you to forgiveness, the way the Lord would have done. If you believe in God you have to go that way. I know that you are a fighter and that you will not give up your life because of what has happened. I think we should pray about it and if you have faith like I do, I know that everything will work out the best they can, because there is still an Almighty God." She launched into prayer for Deidre-Ann and Soliel joined in. She reminded Deidre-Ann of Miss Nellie. *I must call her tomorrow,* she said to herself. *I will never forget her and Slinky's kindness. There must be a God somewhere who provided help for me in my time of need.*

After praying, they talked way into the night and all three fell asleep right there.

Slinky sat in the back of Mr. Lenworth's SUV. It was the first time he had ever driven in such a vehicle but the exhilaration was missing. How could he explain to Deidre-Ann why he had betrayed her? He looked outside at the pleasant scenery. In the country, the trees were so much bigger and lush. The fat green leaves waved happily at them and the animals grazing contentedly seemed not to have a care in the world except when to eat or sleep. But it did nothing to calm the turmoil in his body. A raw wind had sprung up and the cold air nipped at his face and arms, but he didn't mind it, it was much better than the hot city from which he was coming.

The fidgeting of the man beside him caused him to look around. He wished he could sit elsewhere away from this bearded man. He was wearing a sinister scowl on his face which was decorated with scars and holes of different descriptions. His brown and black beard seemed to be hiding secrets within it. The handcuffs on his hands made him uncomfortable. He kept fidgeting and in the process, bounced against Slinky who tried to edge away as far as possible from him without upsetting the man sitting on the other side.

Soon, they got to a small town. There were quite a number of vehicles rushing about in a panic and the people around tried to keep pace with them. The buildings, which were mostly shabby brick structures, stared dully at nothing and everything in particular. Mr. Lenworth pulled over after circling the roundabout. Nathan got out and released the bearded man from the handcuffs. He attached a device inside his shirt and cautioned, "Remember you are flanked on every side; one wrong move and you are in trouble. Remember how to position yourself and make certain you call names and mention the incident or you will be in as much trouble as he is! Since he wants you to come all the way out here to give him information that you can't over the phone or in the city, given that he is too busy to come there, we are only too glad to oblige and follow him wherever he leads." He shook his finger in warning as the man got out of the SUV.

The man walked away, followed by silence. Everyone got back into the vehicle and waited. After about two minutes, a voice came over a machine that Nathan had turned on.

"So Elton, what is so important that you couldn't tell me, but had me come all the way over here?"

"Ah couldn't tell you dat the police a close in on you tail over the phone."

"What you mean close on my tail, how come? What you do wrong now?" There was breathlessness and surprise in the voice.

"Mr. Gayle, they somehow found out what you do to the girl, ah mean, Ann..."

"Shh, shh, don't call any names in here, suppose somebody follow you." He sounded nervous and stopped speaking.

Mr. Lenworth whispered, "I know that voice! I would know that voice anywhere. Jesus saviour, Gayle! Gayle did this to my little girl! You know I am going to kill him. Let me get out of here!" His voice trembled with rage.

Nathan turned off the machine and grabbed him. "You will do no such thing! Leave the law to deal with him! Now shut up so I can get the evidence!" He turned back on the device quickly.

Mr. Gayle was speaking again. "How you know that the police on to us? You did something wrong! After all the money ah pay you to watch and then deal with the case for me, you mess up!"

"No, no, not me! From you rape the girl ah been doing as you say..."

"Shut your mouth, is more money you want! But look at you, you is only a low life gardener. You think I'm going down in this alone! And ah going to get you before they get me! You're in this as well..."

"All ah help you do was hold her, ah didn't do any-thing to her."

"That's all we need!" Nathan turned around to Mr. Lenworth who was opening the door. He grabbed him and before he knew what was happening, snapped a pair of handcuffs on one hand and cuffed him to the steering wheel. "I had an idea this would happen so I came prepared for it! Come officer."

He jumped out of the vehicle, closed the door behind him and walked in the same direction the bearded man had gone.

In a short while he came back with four police officers and Mr. Gayle and Elton handcuffed between them.

Mr. Lenworth screamed obscenities at them as they were ushered into an unmarked police vehicle and driven away.

Mrs. Lindsay went to the door in answer to a knocking on the gate. She did not get many visitors and she wondered who could be out there in the powerful midday sun which had already wilted her plants. They were a little way from the house so she could not make out the faces clearly.

"Who are you? Who do you want?" she asked peering intently at the faces peering back at her.

At that moment, Mr. Lenworth put his finger to his lips cautiously.

Mrs. Lindsay peered some more and then placed her hand over her mouth in surprise. A shy smile spread over her face and without hesitation, she went and opened the gate.

"I do not want Ann to see you before you enter the house," she said in a loud whisper. "If she does, she might refuse to speak to anyone at all."

She hugged her brother and said, "I have many things to discuss with you but not now. However, I must warn you to tread lightly, you are dealing with a very delicate situation. We can only hope for the best and don't expect too much." Her words of warning were enough to set the veins in Mr. Lenworth's neck pumping fiercely. "I remember you vaguely," she said to Nathan. "You must be Ann's police cousin. She told me about you and how much help you have been. She is around the back playing scrabble with my daughter. I will get her." She started off and then stopped. "On second thought, Simon, you and Slinky had better stay hidden, this could be too traumatic for her and undo all that we have been trying to do."

"I think that is a very good idea," Nathan said, sitting on a chair, while Mr. Lenworth and Slinky went into the nearest room where they could overhear everything.

In a few minutes, Mrs. Lindsay returned with Deidre-Ann and Soliel, who was holding her hand tightly. She stopped when she saw Nathan.

"Hi Ann!" Nathan got up and went forward. He stopped and held out his hand. Ann hesitated and then put her hand in his.

"Hi Nathan, I see you have found me!" It was a statement made without malice.

"Yes Ann, we have searched long and hard and finally here you are. I hope we can work things out so that you will be more comfortable and this does not happen again." He looked at her with a real smile, one he had not managed in months.

"How did you find me? Did Slinky tell you where I was?" Deidre-Ann looked him straight in the eyes.

"In fact he did, against his will. If he did not we would have arrested him." Nathan's eyes pleaded with hers, begging for understanding.

"Arrest him, arrest him for what? If it wasn't for him and Miss Nellie I would most likely have died!" She was vehement with her praise.

Mr. Lenworth, listening behind the door, reached out and touched Slinky gratefully. He vowed inwardly to help the boy to get off the street.

"We know all about them and we will talk about them later but first I must ask you a few questions to confirm some evidence. Do you know who did this to you?" He didn't want to ask, but he had to.

"Yes, do you?" Deidre-Ann looked away from him.

"Yes, but we need more information from you."

"That man next door, Mr. Gayle. I thought he was my father's friend." Surprisingly, she was calm; there was not even a tremor in her voice. She looked at Nathan, waiting for him to continue.

"The very same one!" Nathan was so happy. A loud laugh which came from deep down resounded throughout the living room.

"But how did you find out?' Deidre-Ann wanted to know. "I only found out two days ago and I have not told anyone."

"God just allowed us to fit everything together. At the scene of the crime the only thing that could be considered evidence was a small towel. The rain had washed it clean of prints but I took it and put it away nonetheless. A few days ago when I went to visit your mother, I met this most unsavoury character, sweating away and wiping sweat on a cool day. He dropped his rag and when I turned to give him, he was already in his SUV, so I just threw it on the passenger seat beside me. When I was getting out it caught my eye and for some reason I took it up. I remember seeing the pattern somewhere and then it hit me, it was the same pattern I had seen on the towel. I retrieved the first one and matched it, and then sent the second one off for DNA testing." He stopped for a while and cleared his throat, while allowing the details to sink in.

"We started doing checks all over the place and the evidence started pouring in. We found his dental records for a DNA match and arrested 'Beardy' and questioned him. He told us what had happened that night and how Mr. Gayle said he had been watching and planning for that moment for a long time. He inadvertently got information from the helper who was always discussing everything that takes place in your house, not only with the Gayles, but with all the neighbours. When the telephone number was changed, she gave it away."

"I hope he will leave prison only when they carry him out to be buried!" Soliel said, hugging Deidre-Ann.

"I want you to talk to your mother, but before you do so, I want you to hear me out about a little matter. Your father was very instrumental in helping us to solve this case."

"Father! I really do not have a father! Did he tell you where I saw him after all these years?" Despite her aunt's advice, Deidre-Ann was still mad at her father.

"Yes," Nathan said quietly. "He told me and he hates himself for it. As a matter of fact he has changed and will no longer go that route." Nathan's voice was pleading, cajoling.

"He is no good! I realize now that was why he and mummy broke up! I hope he continues to stay away from us." She hissed her teeth furiously.

"Well he won't, he wants to get his family back together," Nathan said.

"Mummy will never talk to him! She hates him!"

"As a matter of fact, he has been trying to talk to her. I don't know how that will go, but I am hopeful that sometime to come, that might be a possibility. Now I beg you, try and forgive and help her to do the same. Ashley is willing and ready."

# CHAPTER FIFTEEN

## *The Salt Returns*

"My God that was a hectic workout. I have not enjoyed myself this much for a long while now," Deidre-Ann said, sitting on one of the stone benches that framed the multi-purpose court.

"It most certainly was," said her classmate sitting beside her. "Do you think the seniors have a chance of winning the netball match this afternoon, Deidre-Ann?" the girl asked.

"If we play as well as we have been playing!" Deidre-Ann replied.

"You mean, if you play as well, as you have been playing. Deidre-Ann you're so good, all those passes and the superb shooting, for someone who claims not to have played this game before, you are extremely good!" The girl's face clearly showed her admiration.

"Well, we had better win because my father said he's coming to watch me play and my mother said that if she gets off early, she will come too. Until that time I am going to the library to copy some material for my SBA because the library will be closed by the time we are finished, and tomorrow evening I won't have the time because I'm leaving right after school so that I can attend the youth rally that the youth organization at my church will be hosting."

She picked up her bag and walked towards the bathroom.

# Other Titles by Colleen Smith-Dennis

- Inner City Girl

- For Her Son

CPSIA information can be obtained
at www.ICGtesting.com
Printed in the USA
BVHW040758101022
648886BV00001B/39